ENDO]

CW00418475

Current of Death
(Oxford eBooks)

A crime writer protagonist in a crime novel will inevitably lead to murder and mystery. This is certainly true in Sylvia Vetta's venture into crime fiction. Her protagonist Alex Hornby has barely finished regretting that her village Thames Reach (a thinly disguised Kennington between Oxford and Abingdon) is in crime terms rather dull, when a walk by the Thames brings her face to face with a floating corpse.

Alex, who has the advantage of knowing the village well, not to mention many of its inhabitants, ends up assisting the police and testing her own fictional detective skills. Deaths, dodgy goings-on, slippery developers, slavery, and Extinction Rebellion all feature in this novel in which Sylvia's passion for her home village shines through. Of course Sylvia says all her characters are pure fiction – but is she telling the truth?

As a crime writer, I advise you never to believe what a crime writer says – after all, deceit and deception is buried in their DNA!

Dodgy goings-on, slippery developers, slavery, and Extinction Rebellion all feature in this crime novel in which Sylvia's passion for her home village shines through.

Peter Tickler: Author of *Blood on the Cowley Road, The Oxford Murders* and other crime fiction

A gripping murder mystery set on the River Thames, Current of Death might be a first venture into the crime genre from a very talented writer, but I hope that it isn't the last.

John Argyle: The Chairman of the Friends of Kennington Library and lockkeeper.

After writing several successful novels, Sylvia Vetta has turned her hand to a new genre. The murder-mystery 'Current of Death' kept me turning the pages, I didn't expect the twist at the end. An interesting mix of characters, a lot like the real Kennington! Looking forward to the next!

Isabella Lindsay: Young resident of Kennington

Sylvia Vetta has been exploring Oxford's waterways for many years so she is perfectly placed to imagine dark deeds in a village she knows well.

Andy Ffrench: Oxford Mail

Food of Love, cooking up a life across gender, class and race.
(Claret Press)

Told with brio and verve, this is an astonishing life story that takes in working-class life in post-war Britain, and the transformation of society in the decades that followed.

Rana Mitter: Professor of the History and Politics of Modern China, the Universities of Oxford and Harvard.

Food of Love is a testimony of zest for life, and compassionate anger at the many forms of injustice in post-war England. Sylvia Vetta's story takes us through her many lives, as she reinvents herself time and time again, rising from the ashes of prejudice, misogyny, racism and greed to renew herself.

Dr Jane Spiro: Professor of Education and TESOL, Oxford Brookes University

Brushstrokes in Time
(Set in the USA and China)(Claret Press)

A Brilliant Compelling Read.

Shrenik Rao: Editor of the Madras Courier

It has to be among my top ten historical novels, certainly of this century. Utterly mesmerising and unforgettable.

Dr Jenny Lewis: internationally renowned poet and teacher (Oxford)

I could not put this page-turner down. As I reached the end just one thought dominated: everyone should read this book. No one I've ever come across has managed to tell the story of modern Chinese politics, arts and society in such accessible, imaginative and compelling a fashion.

Ray Foulk: Founder of the Isle of Wight Festival & author of Stealing Dylan from Woodstock.

Vetta is always accurate with a grasp of vivid detail.

John Gittings: Chief Foreign Correspondent of the Guardian.

Not So Black and White by Sylvia Vetta and Nancy Mudenyo Hunt (Set in London and west Kenya) (The Nasio Trust)

The Book to read after the Black Lives Matter protests.

The Oxford Times

Timey, pacey and personal novel.

Love Reading

Sculpting the Elephant (Set in Oxford and India) (Claret Press)

Found myself totally immersed in the history and culture of a place close to my own origins. The intricate narrative design of two parallel plot lines with their distinctive location and ethos— pulled me deep into the lives of the protagonists. Sylvia Vetta has written a book which fundamentally traces the philosophical and moral dimensions of a journey which crosses racial and religious boundaries.

Professor Rebecca Haque: (Dhaka, Bangladesh)

CURRENT OF DEATH

SYLVIA VETTA

Oxford eBooks

ISBN 978-1-910779-04-0

Cover Illustration by Elizabeth Vetta
Cover Photo by Philip Hind
Illustrations by Antonia, Alexandra and Anastasia Vetta

Produced and published by Oxford eBooks Ltd.

Oxford eBooks

www.oxford-ebooks.com

The characters in this book are fictional and any resemblance to real persons is coincidental.

To the people of Kennington.

FOREWORD

THAMES REACH IS inspired by the village of Kennington where I live. It's an independent sort of place somewhat dwarfed by its famous neighbours. To the north lies academic Oxford with its dreaming spires overshadowing the town with its multicultural east and Cowley car factory where Harry King, the protagonist of my novel *Sculpting the Elephant*, grew up.

Abingdon, which claims to be the longest inhabited town in England, is a few miles south of Kennington. Being overlooked means that villagers have got on with their lives without obvious interference. I've given my village a pseudonym because the characters in *Current of Death* are all fictional. Just one - the volunteer lockkeeper - resembles a genuine Kenningtonian.

The river Thames flows through Oxford past Kennington to Abingdon. Its beauty and force of nature flow through the narrative.

The Cover: The atmospheric photo of the river near Iffley is courtesy of Philip Hind and the water painting by the talented artist, Elizabeth Vetta. The charming illustrations are by Antonia, Alexandra and Anastasia Vetta.

Sylvia Vetta June 2023

CHAPTER 1

STRANGER THAN FICTION

'... DEATH BY natural causes - a heart attack - Giovani's body was found after considerable exertion in a bedroom at the Club ...'

ALEX HORNBY WAS imagining it all, so there had to be more to it than that. She'd just read *The Human Condition* by Hannah Arendt. It left her considering how easy it is to be deceived and to deceive oneself. She wanted to explore that theme in her latest book.

The crime writer arranged time out from writing her as yet nameless novel to meet her new neighbours over coffee and banana bread. Homemade cakes were one of the draws the Library Friends group used to attract people to their monthly author presentations. More sweet delights were features of the community café – *mouth-watering*, but hardly over stimulating.

It was going to be a challenge to make the soporific Thames Reach sound exhilarating. Alex resigned herself to the truth that her village was nothing like her books: it was neither a den of crime nor a hive of anti-social behaviour. She visited the local primary school to hear children read and sometimes to talk about reading for pleasure with year groups. They were so well-behaved that she wondered if she should stir up a little rebellion. A pang of guilt irked her as she visualised her teacher friend, Achla, in her classroom. How could she wish another challenge on her when teaching was such a demanding profession!

Alex's passion for history was not universally welcomed. Her ex-husband claimed that for an author she was not self-aware, and prone to ignoring yawns of boredom when she embarked on yet another story from the distant past. Remembering that comment, she tried to focus on the diversity of nature around them. Thames Reach was only a few miles from the beautiful city of Oxford, squeezed into a narrow track of land between Bagley Woods and the River Thames. But, having described the natural assets of the village to her visitors, she couldn't stop herself.

'The village was a lawless place in the 13th century, when men were frequently assaulted and even killed in Bagley Wood. Even the Prior of the Abbey was carried off into the wood and threatened with a horrible end unless he did the Prior-napper's bidding.'

Her new neighbour brought the flow of words to a halt.

'We chose to move here because it's only a field away from Oxford but still affordable enough to buy a house,' said Cleo. Jo, the husband, looked protectively at his pregnant wife whose athleticism was tempered by a relaxed pose. Her dark hair was cropped, emphasising her deep, enquiring eyes.

He added, 'And we'll have to start thinking about schools soon. I heard the village school here has a good reputation.'

'Oh, my son went there! And my friend, Achla, teaches there,' said Alex. 'It has a good reputation, and deservedly so. It's not just academics, they really help the kids get along too.'

Looking at Cleo, she asked, 'When's it due?'

Cleo smiled and put a hand over her rounded stomach.

'September 20th - just four months to get the house organised and ready!'

Helpful neighbour that she was, Alex handed her a copy of the Good Neighbours brochure and the local magazine, *The Thames Reach Chronicle*.

'Local tradesmen advertise in this, in case you need a plumber or a carpet fitter. We're a large village - there's a surprising number of organisations. Do you have any hobbies?'

'We haven't had a garden before so we could do with some advice,' said Jo. 'Is there a society that could help us?'

'The Horticultural Society isn't just popular: it's the largest in Oxfordshire. I can take you to a meeting if you'd like. New groups interested in wildlife and rewilding have started up, encouraging us to make our gardens bird and insect friendly, installing swift boxes and bee boxes on the church tower, that sort of thing. Last month they even organised a hedgehog-friendly event.'

She giggled. 'Obviously, the hedgehogs were invited.'

'I heard about that,' said Jo. 'They want us to make sure there are ways the prickly creatures can cross our garden. I notice you have a gap in our joining fence but there isn't one on the other side. Come to think of it, we haven't even seen our neighbours at No 46. Are they on holiday?'

Alex hesitated. She didn't want to give a negative

first impression by gossiping, however truthfully, about the neighbourhood.

'Frank is a widower and a District Councillor. He's in Australia visiting his son but he'll be back soon. Best of luck persuading him to have a hedgehog hole, though. He prefers his plants lined up regimental style; he'd have a heart attack if he found so much as a daisy on his lawn!'

Jo, suddenly restless, interjected, 'Thanks, Alex. It's been lovely but we'd better unpack some more boxes. Can we take you up on your offer of rambles around the village? We love walking and we're thinking of getting a dog once we've settled in.'

'If we can manage a dog and a baby,' added Cleo. 'It's long been a dream of Jo's, but I'm not sure I'll manage a lead *and* a pushchair.'

Alex showed them out, having planned the first ramble for the following weekend.

***

On Sunday, she took them to Westwood Park and Bagley Woods. In the seventies and eighties, a lot of deciduous trees had been replaced by rows of commercial conifers. The ancient limes and oaks used to look sad in the shadow of the alien invasion. Alex delighted in the recent changes and said,

'The college, who own the wood, have received a grant to naturalise it, which came with the condition to open it to the public.' Alex then indicated an area where some conifers had recently been felled.

'We call that Den City,' said Alex, pointing to a

family busy building yet another creation out of branches, leaves and bracken. 'When my son was growing up, we had to get permission from the college to walk here but now access is community friendly.' As if to prove the statement, joggers passed by on a nearby track.

'If you love nature,' she continued, 'Thames Reach is a great place to start your family.'

They emerged after a two-mile stroll into Abingdon Way, once part of an ancient route from London to Abingdon, supposedly the oldest inhabited town in England. Most of the neighbouring houses were mock Tudor with open drives, teeming with rich banks of wild flowers and surrounded by ancient trees. Alex glanced at the house opposite. Its front garden had once been a riot of colour but was now a dull wash of grey, paved over for car parking. Cleo saw her expression.

'That sticks out like a sore thumb!'

'Indeed it does,' sighed Alex. 'A local builder, a friend of your neighbour Frank, just had that done a few months ago.'

She pointed to the new three-storey square house with a strange extension at the back. Its entrance was adorned with plastic pillars and, as if that alone wasn't garish enough, was surrounded by a ten-foot high wall topped with barbed wire - interrupted only by the security gates mounted with CCTV cameras.

'Godfrey's grandfather built the large timbered houses in the late thirties and made the family the richest in Thames Reach. But he was liked - he supported the community, especially local sports societies. His grandson somehow got permission to knock down his grandfather's house and build that ugly thing, and felled six ancient trees in the process. He's Thames Reach's eco enemy number one.'

CHAPTER 2

ABINGDON REACHES

THE FOLLOWING SUNDAY, Alex woke at four thirty in the morning with a vision of a character for her latest book. This was usual for her. She stretched out to pick up the notebook she kept by her bedside. As she wrote down the description, it reminded her of someone oddly familiar. But who? It took a few seconds before her sleepy brain sparked with energy. It was as if she had clicked on a cigarette lighter.

Of course! Last week at the community café she'd introduced Cleo and Jo to George Gamble, the architect behind the local campaign to fight back against the erosion of the natural world. Together with his granddaughter, he'd opposed the Council using *Round Up* - a weed killer that penetrates the soil killing everything - and mowing the village verges during the summer. George wouldn't call the plants they wanted to eradicate 'weeds': he rather delighted in them as wild flowers. He'd also organised the opposition to Godfrey's monstrosity and the destruction of the ancient trees. Despite a lengthy petition, it passed the local planning committee. They'd only managed to save one oak, which had felt like a token nod to democracy, the sole purpose of which was to hide the fact that money had triumphed.

'Why did no one at the press complain about that loss?' thought Alex. The local press was a guarantor of some accountability in local government,

especially in planning. She knew first hand. She'd written for local magazines to supplement her meagre novelist's earnings, until the decline of the local press was cemented by the sacking of all their freelancers. The energetic and hardworking young graduates working on *The Oxford Mail* did their best, but most didn't grow up in Oxfordshire, and lacked a depth of personal local knowledge. They had to learn as fast as they could on the job and, considering how few of them were left, provided a good service to the community, *'Why does my brain do that?'* thought Alex. It fell off the branch when I was thinking of George.

George was hard to have a conversation with, though, unless you asked him about a bird. He was a fount of knowledge about local wildlife. She often saw him out with his binoculars and camera. He even kept a jeweller's magnifier in his pocket to examine blossom, lichen and insects close up.

Why the comparison with the dream? The character was much younger than George. It must be the clothes: George cared not a jot about what he wore. In winter, he was nearly always in the same old jeans with an Arran sweater under a waxed jacket. Then the bobble hat – his granddaughter, Carrie, had knitted it for him for a Christmas present at least eight years ago. Carrie was now grown up, twenty at least. But she shared her grandfather's passion. Nearly all the Extinction Rebellion videos, taken in Oxford, had Carrie centre stage. It was a teenage Carrie whom George had tied to the oak tree three years ago to save it. She hadn't worn her red Extinction Rebellion robes for that demonstration: for that one she wore a vast cloak made of leaves.

Alex tossed and turned. She couldn't get back to sleep so, at six am, she decided to shower, have an early breakfast and go for a walk. At that time of the morning, the birdsong alongside Sustran's cycle path was like a thunderous Beethoven symphony.

She arrived at the industrial estate where the Tap Social Movement had a bakery not far from Thames Reach builders' yard. At 8 am, it had just opened. She stopped, downed a coffee and was tempted to consume an *entire* creamy almond croissant. She thought better of it after looking at her waistline. *Still - why not take a day off writing and walk over to Abingdon, have lunch there, go to the concert in St Nic's and return on the bus?* She ordered the croissant.

Alex was not a lover of procrastination. When she had an idea in her head, she wanted to write it down before she forgot, but the sun was shining and the Thames Path beckoned. She headed down the lane and went right towards Lower Radley. Thirty minutes later she had passed the college boat house and glanced across the river towards the Global Retreat. The Hindu group, the Brahma Kumaris leased Harcourt House and grounds from the university. She'd been there on a course of meditation. She liked the group's openness but knew it wasn't for her – a bit too introspective. Odd, considering she was a writer who spent so much time alone - but, as a crime writer, it was to observe people's behaviour in society that she needed to do, rather than look inwards.

Around the next bend, Alex caught site of a heron.

The stately bird stood upright, still and steady on his spindly legs as its sharp eyes scanned the river. The water bird glided upwards with elegant wings outstretched. Dazzling white above, reflected grey in the water beneath as he flew. Without warning, he dived and speared a fish. Alex felt privileged. What a good idea it had been to extend her walk.

Thames Reach may not be exciting in the way of her novels set in nearby Oxford, but that had been magical. Alex's last book was set in East Oxford, noted for its diversity and yet, over the last two decades, Thames Reach had become quietly diverse as well. To be the first black resident of the village had taken some courage. Her son had been the first black pupil at the primary school, but now every race and creed was represented. In East Oxford diversity was always on display. There were Polish, Middle Eastern, Indian, Chinese and Caribbean restaurants and takeaways. The rhythms from nightclubs, the mosque and the modern Pentecostal church loved by the residents of African ancestry were distinct and yet somehow complementary.

There was nothing like that in Thames Reach, but new residents soon felt at home. In the early twentieth century, the manor estate had been broken up and the land auctioned in lots. When Alex moved in, cabin-like homes were dotted around the village. Artisans out of Oxford had built them for themselves. That streak of independence was what made the village special. Everyone could live how they liked and be accepted, so long as they didn't do it ostentatiously.

Alex took out her notebook and wrote: *Suspicious*

of show-offs.

A noise jerked her out of her thoughts. She became aware of someone nearby. It was George Gamble. He'd clearly just witnessed the same heron.

'Wow!' said Alex, 'Did you get a picture of that dive?'

George nodded and then pointed downstream.

'Approach quietly and you'll see some kingfishers.'

Alex followed his gaze to a bushy outcrop beyond where a gracious whispering green willow dipped its fingers lightly in the river. It wasn't a kingfisher, but a Canada goose which launched into the sky, sending ripples over the Radley side of the river. Alex said goodbye to George and continued along the Thames Path. There was a gaggle of eight geese around the next bend in the river as she approached Abingdon. One of them seemed to be pecking at something near the bank among the reeds. When she drew nearer, Alex reached for her binoculars to take a closer look and almost dropped them.

She staggered back and broke her fall by landing on a convenient log. *She was imagining it.* A vivid imagination - that's what comes of writing crime fiction. Maybe that was a sign that she should change genre? She closed her eyes and took a deep breath. There was an inlet twenty metres away. She stepped carefully onto the edge that protruded into the river and again took out her binoculars. This time there was no convenient log and she fell forward into the water. It was less than a foot deep in the sandy spot, so only the bottom of her trousers and the sleeves of her jacket got wet as she broke her fall.

Alex clenched her fists and made herself look. Those were clothes and bloodless fingers. She had *not* imagined it – that was a BODY.

CHAPTER 3

DEJA VU?

ALEX HAD DESCRIBED the scene in front of her in so many books. There was a taped-off area. Anyone approaching was denied access to the path which was covered with a tent, and forced to turn around and retrace their steps. Before they went back the way they came, they were questioned and their contact details taken down by a uniformed officer.

Moving around meticulously were men and women dressed in the same white zombie-like suits which covered them head to toe. You could only guess at the gender of the person wearing it from their gait. A man and a woman approached her. No problem there, as they were wearing ordinary clothes.

'I'm Chief Inspector Ranjit Singh and this is my sergeant, Kate Farr.'

He held out a hand to shake.

'I need to ask you a few questions - I'm sorry for the urgency and for keeping you here when you're probably suffering from shock. Nothing can prepare you for a discovery like this.'

Alex had written similar words so many times that she almost smiled. Detective Sergeant Kate Farr looked hard at Alex and thought: *The portrait picture in your books is poised, hair straightened. The woman in front of me is casually dressed and her hair part-braided. But those dark eyes – no mistaking them.*

'I know who you are. I've read your books. You're

the local crime fiction writer, Alex Hornby.' said Kate out loud.

'You're correct. Most of my books are set in Oxford and London, but I live in Thames Reach. It never seemed like the place for crime. It's been years since I've seen a community policeman in the village. I presumed that Thames Valley Police didn't regard it as an area worth policing,' replied Alex.

The Chief Inspector looked at her, then Kate.

'Books aside, fill me in on your movements this morning and how you discovered the body. Then Kate can drive you to the station to take your written statement.'

Alex described finding Godfrey Price, although she hadn't realised who he was until the policeman in a diving suit extricated him from the dense reeds and fished him out of the river. The police were keeping mum about it, but this didn't appear to be an accidental drowning. There were a few seconds when Alex saw that his legs had been tied together. She remembered thinking - *but no bricks tied to the other end of the rope.*

Alex asked Kate about it once they were in the car.

'Could there have been one and it had come loose?'

'I'm not supposed to discuss any details. All I'll say is that you're a good observer.' Alex took that as **yes**, nothing that would have held the body down.

They drove to the station in Kidlington where she retold her story and affirmed that the only person she'd passed by was George Gamble. Kate wrote everything down and Alex signed each page. She added that she recognised the body of local builder

Godfrey Price. Kate then volunteered to drive her home and on the way, asked Alex what she knew about him.

Alex said: 'He's currently the most unpopular man in the village since he destroyed his grandfather's house in Abingdon Way to build a fortress, cutting down some ancient trees in the process.'

'*Currently* sounds apt given where I found the body. A lot of people are angry, but I can't imagine any of them wanting to kill him. They're green activists, not violent killers.'

'Maybe, but we've seen animal rights activists send bomb threats to scientists who work in the Oxford lab that experiments on them. It's not outside the realm of possibility. You mentioned Godfrey's grandfather. Is he still alive?'

'No, he died about three years ago. Godfrey inherited the house after that. If Alfred were still alive, he'd never have let him destroy it.'

'What about the rest of the family?

'Godfrey's on his second marriage. His first wife was a local girl, Carol. They'd been together since secondary school. She was a bit of a wallflower, but a good mother to their two children. Their son, Kevin, works for his father...

'I'm talking as if he's still alive! When Godfrey and Carol divorced, the daughter Angela broke contact with her father and went to live in London. Carol moved into a flat in Rose Hill and Angela visits her mother quite often. I know because before she left for London, we were both members of Thames Reach Am Dram Society.'

'Right. What do you know about the divorce?'

'Godfrey changed once he grew the business - became arrogant. He stopped volunteering at the boys' football club and started to spend more time entertaining wealthy businessmen and politicians and stopped being faithful to Carol.'

'How did she react to that?' asked Kate.

'I don't think she minded that much until he started to flout it openly, taking Samantha everywhere with him instead of her. He humiliated her by getting a near neighbour of mine, Frank Foreman, to escort her while he danced with or sat next to Samantha at functions. I guess you'd describe Samantha as a Barbie-looking bimbo but she has more brains than she lets on. They married last year in Las Vegas. Oh, and Carol's mother Margaret still lives in the village, but was found wandering around a few weeks ago. She appears to be getting dementia.'

After the interview, Kate drove Alex home. The mood became more relaxed than it had been in the police station.

'This must seem a bit eerie for you. In *'Parson's Deathly Pleasure'* a body is found naked in reeds in the Cherwell. You must have visualised events like this one before.'

'You're right, but this was different –shocking. For me, plotting a crime thriller is an intellectual exercise. I can't do Scandie Noir or sadist violence against women. Maybe *can't* isn't the right word - I WON'T is more accurate. I worry whether that kind of literature makes heinous crimes against women seem normal. I'm more interested in developing characters and working out what motivates them to commit a crime, and not all my books are murder mysteries. Fraud, blackmail, embezzlement and exploitation can be interesting to write about and revealing too. Dickens was good on those. So, you've actually **read** my books!'

'Yes and I'm waiting for the next one. As a detective, understanding motivation is important. It's not first on our list. Establishing how the murder was done, forensics and who was in a position to do it come first. Understanding the victim is important and you're good at that.'

Kate parked outside Alex's house in Woodland Road. For some reason, Alex was pleased it was an unmarked police car.

'Thanks. I'll invite you to the launch of my next book, although reading crime novels, sounds like a busman's holiday for you. I do hope you can find who did this.' As she unlocked the door, she turned and saw her on the phone, presumably reporting to Ranjit. Kate looked annoyed and clenched her fist.

'Hmm' thought Alex. *'What has he said to her to make her react like that?*

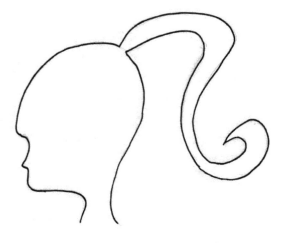

CHAPTER 4

BARBIE GIRL

'SOMETIMES I WONDER why I chose this job,' said Ranjit, letting out a pensive sigh. Kate hoped he'd say more. After a few minutes of silence he said, 'I wake up at night reliving horrific scenes from all the road accidents I've had to deal with. When I informed the relatives, I tried to force myself to forget. This is different. This is my first non-domestic murder. Well, we're treating it as murder, but until we have the pathologist's report, we can't absolutely rule out suicide. After all, his hands weren't tied and the injury to the head could have happened on the rock in the river where we found him.'

'So what do we tell his wife? Unexplained drowning?'

'Sounds about right. We need her to do the formal identification. I expect you believe your author mate, Alex but I want to make certain the body is Godfrey Price.'

Kate was beginning to regret her remark about Alex's books.

They parked the car outside Godfrey's fortress, pressed the intercom button and waited. After two minutes they tried again. No answer.

'How do you get into this place? You can't even scale the walls – look at all that barbed wire. Call in for a phone number for Samantha Price.'

Five minutes later, Samantha answered her mobile

and the gates slowly drew apart. When she appeared at the front door, she was sporting a tightly wrapped towel and, Kate suspected, nothing else. They showed her their badges.

'Sorry,' she said, sounding unenthused by the intrusion. 'I was in the swimming pool when the bell rang. Come in.'

Samantha showed them into a vast living room and pointed to the deep white leather sofas, excusing herself with a nonchalant, 'Mind if I dress?'

While she was away, Ranjit got up and fetched a dining chair from the other end of the room. 'I can't do this sprawled out like a frog.'

When Samantha returned, a pregnant woman with dark hair was with her.

'This is my physio, Cleo. We've been working out and were just cooling off with a dip in the pool.'

Kate glanced at Ranjit, wondering if he was thinking the same as she was. They were there about a watery dip of a different nature.

Samantha had let down her silver blonde hair and put on dangling earrings over a low-cut, peacock blue mini-dress.

'Can I get you a drink?' she asked.

'We're not allowed while on duty, but thank you for offering.'

'Do you mind if I have one? But, it'll be mostly soda and only a taste of gin,' asked Samantha, reaching for a bottle on the bar. Kate looked at her seriously.

'I think you should sit down. Please, sit.'

It finally dawned on Samantha that this was not a social call. Ranjit faced Cleo.

'Would you mind leaving the room please? We'll tell you when we've finished.'

He turned to Samantha after Cleo had left.

'Are there any family members in the house?

'No' said Samantha. 'My husband Godfrey is out and,' she tapped on her tummy, 'this little one needs another six months to cook.'

'When did you last see your husband?' asked Kate.

'We were woken at an ungodly hour by a phone call. Before five o'clock I think. I'm sure he said he had to go to the yard. We'd partied into the early hours, so I groaned and went to sleep again but I'm surprised he hasn't called me.'

'I'm sorry, Mrs Price, but we have bad news for you. We believe that your husband drowned a few hours ago in the Thames near Abingdon. To be absolutely sure that it is him, we need you to identify the body.'

Samantha paled, voice quivering as she shot back, 'That can't be true. You're lying! Goldie's a good swimmer, and why would he swim in the Thames when we have a perfectly lovely swimming pool?'

She grabbed her phone and started to dial, presumably Godfrey's phone. There was no ringing at the other end.

'No!' Samantha screamed and put her hands over her mouth. Katie thought she looked a different Samantha from the woman who'd ushered them in so arrogantly. She appeared distraught, genuinely grieving.

'Is there someone you'd like with you? Who can we call? Godfrey's parents?' asked Ranjit.

Samantha held tightly onto the arms of the chair

and stumbled with her words

'They ... they've retired - Marbella. Goldie's son Kevin's lives near by but he doesn't like me much. I suppose he tolerates me, unlike that bitch Angela.'

Ranjit raised an eyebrow, 'Angela?'

'Godfrey's daughter by his first wife. She hasn't talked to Goldie since we married. Angela lives in Brixton and Carol in Rose Hill.'

'Does *your* mother live close by?

Samantha stared to cry.

'I miss her so much it's like a physical pain. My mother died soon after I met Goldie. His grandfather died around the same time. Grief connected us. I'm an only child. My charming father abandoned us when I was a teenager. I've no idea where he is.'

For the first time, Kate was feeling sorry for Samantha.

'Can I bring in my physio? I like Cleo.'

Kate surmised that Samantha had a light bulb moment. Her seemingly rich life was hollow. The closest friend she could think of at this time was her paid physiotherapist.

CHAPTER 5

A FRIEND IN NEED

ALEX WAS SURPRISED when Cleo knocked on her door at 6 o'clock, looking distressed.

'Am I disturbing you? Are you about to eat supper?'

'Don't worry about that. Come on in and tell me what's the matter.' She led Cleo into the lounge, where she sank into a seat looking exhausted but relieved.

'You remember last week, when you took us for a walk and showed us the fortress house? Well, I've been inside it today.'

Alex's surprised expression said it all.

'I've worked as a personal trainer at the Thameside Hotel gym for a couple of years. In the past six months, I've had a client called Samantha. I told her that I was leaving to go freelance – I want more flexibility once the baby's here – and she asked me if I'd continue as her personal trainer. She told me about the gym and swimming pool in her house. She's pregnant and thought it could be fun as I am too. When she gave me her address, I knew right away where it was.'

'We were both in the pool when the bell rang. At first, Samantha ignored it. When her phone rang, she thought it was her husband Godfrey but it turned out to be the police. Alex, Godfrey is dead.'

Alex was holding a pen in her hand and she clicked it then apologised.

'Cleo. You must think I'm a cold person - not reacting to that news but you see − I already knew.

It was me who found the body in the Thames this morning.'

'Alex! What happened? How are you?'

Alex told her the whole story and that, considering she was a crime writer, she found it hard to understand why she had felt shaken to the core.

'So you were with Sam when the police arrived to tell her. How did she react?' asked Alex.

'Alex, I've just come back from the morgue. Samantha had to identify his body.'

Cleo looked distraught.

'She has no parents and is completely on her own. I don't think she has any real friends. They've thrown lots of parties but when I suggested that she gets someone to stay with her, she cried. I thought she was a tough cookie but I couldn't have been more wrong. Then she asked *me* to go with her to the morgue. I wanted to say no. They say that babies in the womb react to how a mother is feeling. But she's pregnant too and has no one - absolutely no one. Oh Alex, it was *horrible*. I'm worried about her.'

Cleo started to cry. Alex went over and hugged her and held her for a few minutes.

'You did a kind thing, Cleo. And kindness is the most under– appreciated virtue. Your baby will know that her mother is good person.'

'I don't know why I'm crying. I've never met Godfrey, and by all accounts I probably wouldn't have liked him but you know, Samantha was not faking it. She left that morgue ashen and started to sob and sob. She said, 'I can't believe it but it's him, Cleo. It's Goldie.' She's grieving and has no-one to comfort her.'

'I'm glad you've been able to cry. Now, you need to eat and then sleep; but tomorrow, I'll come with you to see her. But you should be aware that if Samantha finds out that I know Angela, she'll probably throw me out.'

Alex thought hard. Did Angela know? Should I ring and tell her? Surely the police will tell Godfrey's ex and his children?

CHAPTER 6

FAMILIES

RANJIT'S PARENTS HAD hoped he'd become a doctor, but he was uncomfortable with blood and vomit. That was an understatement. As he left the lab where he'd watched the post-mortem on Godfrey Price, he felt queasy but at least he didn't have to wield the knife.

As he headed home, he switched the car radio to the BBC Asian Network. He couldn't face the news of wars and aggression everywhere.

'Crazy!' he thought, 'Not how most people would expect a policeman to react.'

The Bollywood music playing was from the fifties and much loved by his grandparents. Despite his desire to escape talk of violence, it prompted visions of them and the trauma they'd experienced. His great grandfather had been in the British Indian Army and died of typhoid at the siege of Kut Al Amara during the First World War. His six month old grandmother never met him. His grandparents on his father's side were on the wrong side of the border at the Partition of India. They'd lost all their possessions, but escaped with their lives. They never talked about what they'd seen on that long trek from Lahore to Jullundur. His father knew what racism was as a schoolboy in Birmingham in the sixties.

The idea around the uniform had been part of the attraction of the police force—Ranjit felt guilty that he'd stopped wearing a turban. Kirpal, his bus driver father was serious about his Sikh religion and always wore an immaculate one. An added incentive was that his university expenses were paid for, so long as he entered the force after graduating.

After a few years in London, he thought he'd made a mistake. The racism in the force was felt not just by black boys on the street, but also by non-white officers. He suppressed an image of himself as a greenhorn copper being surrounded in the gents, mocked and pushed from one so called *colleague* to another in a game of 'n' rugby. Orders from above were to become diverse, more representative of twenty first century London. As a graduate recruit, they couldn't side–line him completely. They eventually allowed him to become a detective sergeant long after white graduates who'd entered when he did. They pushed him into traffic and domestic crimes which made an upgrade to Chief Inspector unlikely. He'd been rejected for promotion every time he applied, due to 'lack of experience'.

On a whim, he applied for the post in the Thames Valley and he'd expected a similar negative outcome. He was still pinching himself every time he entered the station, making sure he wasn't living in Alice's Wonderland. The Chief Constable was a woman, and Ranjit wondered if that was why he felt part of a team here. It was easier for him than for his Muslim colleague, Kamal, because Ranjit enjoyed a drink. After a hard week, he could let go of the tension with colleagues over a pint in the local. Thinking about *uniform*, he looked at himself in his blue suit and laughed. He was lucky too with his Detective

Sergeant. Kate was in her mid-forties and seemed capable and diligent. Ranjit was surprised to learn that she was single. She was an attractive woman. On duty her red hair was pulled tightly back and wound in a severe looking bun, but with it loose, he imagined she'd look like one of those Pre-Raphaelite muses in the Ashmolean.

***

The next day, Kate handed him the report. Having attended the post-mortem, he knew what most of what it would say.

Godfrey Price had died from drowning but he hadn't been awake when he went into the river. He'd been drugged with an overdose of insulin. Godfrey was not a diabetic, but that didn't make much difference in the grand scheme of things. Insulin was a drug that could easily be stolen or acquired. In itself, that didn't prove murder, but - if Price wanted to commit suicide and was going to inject himself, he could have done that at home and left a note. With his new-found wealth and influence and a young wife expecting his baby, why would he do that? Quite frankly, his death was far too suspicious not to be treated as murder. But who had a motive to do it?

***

Kate and Ranjit sat at the back in Chancellor and Jones' office while Clive Jones read the last will and testament of Godfrey Alfred Price. They had agreed to focus on different targets. He asked Kate to watch

Samantha and Angela while he watched the men.

Samantha inherited the house but that was it, no income and no mention of the unborn child. Given that the will was written before it was conceived, the latter was of no surprise. Price's attitude to his daughter Angela was clear: not a mention, *zilch*. Kate noticed that while Angela looked sad, she didn't appear surprised.

Kevin was left the business and his parents some flats in Spain.

Clive Jones's voice sounded more approving as he read,

'For my grandchildren, substantial investments will mature when they are eighteen. I leave £10,000 from my personal account to Thames Reach Boys' Football Club, to be used to fund the Godfrey Price Trophy for the player of the year.

'There's an additional item I need to mention. It concerns a purchase that postdates the will,' said Clive with a touch of hesitation in his voice.

'Last year, Godfrey bought land near Radley College. A few days before he died, he came here and transferred ownership of it to his son, Kevin and his friend Frank Foreman. I'm not sure that he had time to tell you he'd done that.'

Kevin looked surprised, but Ranjit noticed that the Councillor didn't react at all.

***

Back at the station, Kate and Ranjit started their Investigation Board. On it were pics of Godfrey

Price and his wives, his two children, his parents Susan and John Price and ex mother-in-law, Margaret Pugh. Above them was a map of the local area. At the heart of it was the meandering Thames, interrupted by Iffley and Sandford Locks, and highlighted close by the river, to the south, was Godfrey's house in Thames Reach and his business in the industrial estate situated a few hundred yards from Sandford Lock. Ranjit addressed the team.

'Our victim is local builder, Godfrey Price. His body was found tangled in reeds and bushes in the Thames, a mile from Abingdon. Before we think of *who*dunnit, we need to work out the 'HOW' dunnit. How did his body get there? It's impossible to get a vehicle anywhere close to that spot. Nor were there any indications that he'd been dragged into the river at that point. He'd been injected with insulin. He was not dead when he went into the water, but he was certainly unconscious. That amount of insulin injected may well have killed him if his body had not ended in the river but the verdict of the post mortem is death by drowning. Any comments?'

The silence was broken by PC Veronica Chen, 'Bikes and motor bikes with a trailer could access the Thames Path. Could the body have been carried on one?

'Good suggestion - but if he was transported there, how would you explain no drag marks from the Thames Path to the bank of the river? Motor bike or cycle tracks carrying a heavy body would've left deeper indentations than the average cyclist on the Thames Path, and forensics found none.'

'What if he was dropped from a boat?

'That sounds feasible, but could only a punt or a kayak have come that close in to the bank? It's less than a half metre deep where we found the body. DC Jordan, research the Thames, its currents and how close a motorboat would need to get for the body to end up entangled in the reeds. Richard, see if there's any CCTV anywhere along the river between Oxford and Abingdon that could give an idea of river traffic and people on the Thames Path between 5 and 7am on Sunday. Then there is the drug used. Could any of the family and other members of the board of Thames Reach Builders Ltd have had access to insulin?' DC Jordan, look into that too. Richard can help you on both those tasks,' he added, looking at Richard Smith, their civilian IT expert.

Then Ranjit pointed to the board.

'If our victim was female, our prime suspect would be her partner. In this case, I think we can rule out Samantha. From the will, it's clear that she had nothing to gain. Price didn't even have life insurance. She's expecting his baby and seemed genuinely pleased about it. It was virtually the first thing she told us even though it's not obvious yet.'

Kate nodded her agreement. Her colleagues looked thoughtful as Ranjit continued, 'With male victims, 18.5% are killed by a friend or an acquaintance and a further 9% by someone they know. I suggest that we concentrate on that aspect of Price's life first. This doesn't have the hallmarks of a stranger attack. It looks premeditated. Any comments?'

Kate asked, 'What about Angela? Could she be

resentful? Nothing left to her. Maybe she thought he hadn't changed his will but was concerned that he was about to do that, given his recent marriage to Samantha.'

'That's worth following up. Can you do that Kate? Find out what you can about her circumstances and where she was on Sunday. Either your suspicion will get legs or we can rule her out. Can you talk to her mother, Carol too - same aim?'

'There's another woman on the board. She lives in the village on Woodland Road,' said Kate.

'Her name is Margaret Pugh. She's Carol's mother, grandmother to Angela and Kevin, great-grandmother to Kevin's children. We sent a constable to inform her of the death of her son-in -law. She didn't seem upset by the news, but Samantha did say she has dementia – visiting her may be a waste of our time,' said Ranjit.

'I'll go to Price's yard to talk to Kevin. But first we need to look into the business. Can you do that?' looking at Richard Smith, 'Lots of overtime for you. Report your findings to me – you can interrupt me at any time.'

'Now we come to suspects beyond the family. There's plenty of village gossip about Price. Locals are angry about the damage he's done to the environment and the house he's built. They don't see it as being in keeping with the neighbourhood. Jordan and Chen – knock on doors in Abingdon Way. Get the lowdown on comings and goings as well as people who quarrelled with him.'

'Alex Hornby described Godfrey as Thames Reach's number one Eco villain.'

'Look out for Spiderman or woman,' joked Ranjit 'but, on second thoughts forget what Kate just said and concentrate on fact rather than fiction.'

CHAPTER 7

INSIDE THE FORTRESS

ALEX AND CLEO rang the bell of the Price fortress. Samantha must have seen who was calling as the gates opened quickly this time. Alex was curious to see inside. The first thing she tended to do was peruse bookshelves. You could tell a lot about a person by what they read. The ground floor was open-plan and as far as she could see, not a single book in sight. There was a vast coffee table on which glossy lifestyle and fashion magazines were laid out. At the far end was a large state of the art kitchen - but with no signs that much cooking was done there. Shortly afterwards, a red-eyed Samantha joined them, as if she'd been crying just minutes ago. She muttered a few cursory niceties and offered coffee, which Alex and Cleo accepted.

They talked about the funeral. What else was there to talk about? Samantha confessed that she had no idea when the body would be released, and she hoped her in-laws would take charge of arrangements.

'Where are they staying?' asked Alex.

'With Kevin.' Samantha looked distraught at Cleo.

'Cleo, I … I can't employ you anymore. This half empty house is mine' she waved her arms pointing to the walls of the house, 'but no means to maintain it, to pay the bills. I've no income of my own. My mum lived in a council house and had nothing to leave me. I gave up my job on the makeup counter at Boots when I married Goldie. I could go back to that but the salary would be a drop in the ocean. I don't know what I'm going to do.'

Samantha's eyes began to water again. Before they could spill over into fresh tears, Cleo gave her hug.

'Listen. *Look at me*. You don't need to worry about paying me. I'll carry on for friendship's sake. Let's think about this house … Thames Reach isn't North Oxford but even so the property must be worth over a million, maybe two? Start by getting it valued.'

Samantha, sniffling, looked grateful.

***

Accompanied by Veronica Chen, Kate headed off for Rose Hill where Carol lived in a flat near the local school. Conveniently, she lived on the first floor. They knocked and waited. No-one came so Kate knocked on the door of the flat opposite. A young mother answered it.

'Oh, trust me, she's in. She rarely goes out. Her son orders her groceries and they get delivered.'

Kate tried again. This time she knocked hard and shouted 'Police!'

The door opened a fraction. It was on a chain. Frightened eyes peered at her. Kate put on her most comforting smile and held up her badge.

'Mrs Price, can we come in please? We need to talk to you.'

Coming in was not easy. Once the chain was removed, they had to inch their way between boxes stacked on either side of the passage that led to the kitchen. Kate saw that every surface was covered with china and glass, biscuit tins and bottles. Carol opened a door on the left. The cramped sitting room was marginally less cluttered than the rest of the house but, even so, there were piles of books and newspapers on every chair. Hardly any light penetrated the window thanks to the sill being lined with overgrown house plants. The flat felt dusty but, mercifully, not dirty. It was the opposite to the sterile, empty palace that was the Price Fortress.

'Can we sit?' asked Kate.

Carol nodded so the constable cleared books and papers from two chairs and they sat down. Kate took in Carol's appearance. Her hair was grey and a long time had passed since it was cut but her eyes were beautiful. Kate looked at her notes. Carole was 57 but she looked more like 70. The contrast with her successor, the ever-elegant Samantha, couldn't have been more extreme.

'Mrs Price, I assume Kevin told you about the death of his father?'

Carol nodded.

'Does your daughter know?'

Carol nodded.

'Mrs Price, we suspect foul play so we have to ask everyone who knew your ex-husband where they were last Sunday.'

Carol nodded.

'Where were you, Mrs Price?

She looked surprised. She murmured one word: 'Here.'

'When did you last see your daughter?'

'Saturday.'

'Does she stay with you when she comes to Oxford?'

Carol shook her head.

'Where does she stay?'

'Jane Morris.'

'Who is she?' asked PC. Chen.

'They were school friends. Jane lives in Thames Reach.'

Kate looked relieved at getting a more than one-word answer to her questions. It didn't seem like Carol was being uncooperative. Kate decoded that Carol had got out of practice talking to people. Indeed, she gave her Angela's address and phone number and that of her friend, Jane. She decided not to press her for now but instead said,

'Thank you, Mrs Price. That's helpful. We may well need to talk to you again. Can you give me your phone number? Next time, I'll make an appointment and not take you off-guard.'

Carol looked appreciative and wrote down her mobile number. Back at the station, she wrote up her notes and proceeded to report in person to Ranjit.

'I don't think she is capable of murder and I believe the neighbour. She rarely leaves that claustrophobic flat. Maybe she suffers from Agoraphobia? We could ask her GP. I imagine her daughter must be upset seeing her mother in those circumstances. I wonder how she came so badly out of the divorce? I'd like to talk to her mother, Margaret, about it. She'd have an opinion.'

'Margaret used to be active and well thought of in the village – a force to be reckoned with. After her husband died, she fundraised for cancer research. She even ran the London Marathon in support of it. If you google her name, lots of Oxford Mail articles come up from eight to ten years ago.'

'But that was ten years ago and now she has dementia. It's sad how a person, even a strong personality disappears once Alzheimer's sets in,' said Ranjit.

'You need to be aware that Councillor Frank Foreman – the one who inherited some land, lives opposite her and doesn't like Margaret. Alex says she's the kind of woman who has opinions and that Frank and some of his fellow councillors don't like women with opinions. They didn't like all the publicity she generated. Frankly, it's hard to imagine that she and Carol are mother and daughter,' said Kate.

'That's a lot of Alex says *this* and Alex says *that*,' teased Ranjit. 'Maybe we should hand over the investigation to her?'

Kate tried to grin at the tease. Something about it struck a nerve.

'We could call on her Inspector Parker,' was her attempt at levity.

'You can have a go at interviewing Margaret but if she has dementia, I'm not sure her testimony will be reliable. So, start with the granddaughter.'

'Shall I visit her in Brixton?'

'Yes, but can you do that one on your own? This investigation needs all of us to work flat out. It's not going to be easy. There are no fingerprints or DNA, no murder weapon and we can't even be sure of how and where he was killed. There are no obvious suspects who would hate him enough to kill him. I couldn't have imagined a worse case than this one to be in charge of for my first murder investigation.'

A minute later, Kate left his office, calling Angela to set up an interview.

***

Meanwhile, Ranjit asked Richard Smith if he'd found anything on Thames Reach Builders, wanting to know as much as he could before visiting Kevin at the yard.

'I can't say I've found anything of significant interest yet, Sir. Their accountants are respectable and they've had no trouble with HMRC. I've compared them with Northmoor Construction. They're similar size firms and both do small-to-medium scale developments but Thames Reach makes way more profit than Northmoor. That could mean something.'

'Well done. See if you can get an idea if there are any legitimate reasons for the difference. Then I'll go and have a few words with Kevin Price. He's the main beneficiary of his father's will and by all accounts Godfrey could be a bit of bully. Is that motive enough?'

CHAPTER 8

CONFRONTATIONS

ALEX COULDN'T HELP herself. She accompanied Cleo on her next visit to Samantha. After all, wouldn't being involved in a real crime help her writing?

Samantha was in a distressed state. Cleo made her sit down and prepared a cup of camomile tea. She felt sure that if it wasn't for her, Samantha would have been tempted to pour herself an alcoholic drink.

'You know how you suggested I got a valuation? Well, Godfrey's solicitors are also estate agents so I called them in. Mr Jones came with the assessor. I explained that I only needed an approximate valuation, I wouldn't necessarily need to sell, if I can get equity release. But I wanted to know how easy it would be to sell. Clive was embarrassed. It appears that no. 1 Abingdon Way wasn't entirely Godfrey's to leave me. Clive had received a visit from Burim Marku, the Albanian builder. When he heard of Godfrey's death, he came to claim his half of the land. He showed him deeds claiming he is joint owner.' She reached for a well-used handkerchief, dabbing at the corners of her eyes.

'Mr Jones apologised because they appear genuine. Godfrey never told me about it. Challenor and Jones should have been given copies of the new deed. It was only signed six months ago, not long before we moved in. The document is held by Marku's solicitors. Clive asked if he could find Godfrey's copy here or at the office. It means that I can't sell without Marku's permission. Cleo, what am I going to do? I can't afford to live here without any means to support myself.'

'Maybe we should meet this Mr Marku? Perhaps he could buy you out. In the meantime, why not do some Air B&B? The swimming pool and gym alone will make it desirable,' suggested Alex.

Samantha ran over to Alex and gave her a hug. Alex felt a tad embarrassed.

***

Once back home, Alex took out Kate's card. She gave her a ring and told her the news about Burim Marku being part owner of no.1 Abingdon Way. Kate sounded quietly impressed.

'That's actually something we weren't aware of. I ought to thank you, Alex. I owe you one. The Chief Inspector is on his way to the office of Thames Reach Builders, I'll ring him about your finding.'

***

The timing of Kate's call couldn't have been better. Ranjit walked into Thames Reach builders' yard to see an angry Burim Marku taking Kevin by his lapels, right up close in his face, and shouting obscenities. Ranjit assumed it was Marku anyway, as he had an eastern European accent. The Albanian clearly didn't welcome whatever Kevin's response was because he drew back a fist. Kevin was prepared and avoided the full force of the blow by escaping Marku's hold with a well-timed shove. Before the tussle could escalate into an all-out brawl, Ranjit separated them and thrust his police ID in their faces.

'In view of what I've just witnessed, gentlemen, I'd prefer to interview you both at the station.'

It looked like Kevin was going to object. He saw Mandy, his secretary, staring out from the office window alongside three workers who had just disembarked from a white van. He shrugged.

'I assume I can come in my own car?'

Ranjit agreed. Marku was given the privilege of their unmarked police car. At the station, they were escorted to separate interview rooms.

As it turned out, Kate had not left for London. She joined Ranjit in the corridor joining the interview rooms.

'Angela is an intensive care nurse, Sir, and is working a twelve-hour shift today. I've arranged to see her tomorrow afternoon. You realise that means that she has access to insulin?'

'Interesting. Help me with these interviews. I suggest we start with Marku.'

***

After the usual procedures, Ranjit started in a subdued, almost friendly tone.

'It looks like we arrived just in time to stop you causing serious injury to Mr Price. What was that all about?''

'We had – how do you call it? A business arrangement. I trusted him, but he a lying toad.'

Marku muttered a curse in Albanian, presumably something particularly offensive.

'Tell us about this arrangement.'

'Look, I speak English okay but not too good for this. I try.'

Marku was a hefty man and looked uncomfortable in the narrow chair. He stretched out his legs under the table and looked straight at Ranjit.

'You know – yea, that Godfrey owns 1 Abingdon Way? The plot is big, at front of two roads. Godfrey, he asked me to build the walls, the roof, drains and guttering of his new house. He paid me but not in cash. I need a house for *my* family. Godfrey said I can build it on the plot where it opens on St Lawrence's Rd. See, he no like gardening. I help him with decking and gravel and he say he happy to lose the rest of the garden. And he promised to help me. Get the right papers. How you say? 'Planning permission?'

'We've been given to understand that you are joint owner of Abingdon Way,' said Kate.

'Not the *house* - the land. What use to me if I can't build? My savings - all spent to buy materials and pay the workers to make that house for him. His business, Thames Reach Builders, finished everything inside.'

Marku let out a loud sigh.

'It was a shock – a big shock −Godfrey dead. I see Kevin and say how I am sorry. Then I start to worry what this mean for me. I ask my solicitor.'

'I go to the council to see – what's the word? The *list* for the meeting?

Ranjit suggested 'the agenda?'

'Yes, that's it.' Marku sighed again and put his head

in his hands. When he looked up, he said,

'Godfrey not keep his promise. My solicitor say joint ownership of the land - not doubt. He explain to me joint ownership. The form for the permission to build my house must to be signed by both owners. Godfrey's death means that is Samantha. You see my problem?'

'Take your time. You're doing well. So you tell us,' said Ranjit.

'Okay. I live on houseboat. My savings they are lost if I can't build that house. I want bring my wife and son here. My friends here worked hard and started businesses. They do well and I want to be like them. Knowing how things done in this country - that is hard for me—very hard. I needed Godfrey. He said permission easy-peasy. His friend Frank would see to it. I believed him. I trusted him. But now he's gone.'

'I went see Kevin for advice. He say he knew nothing. His father not told him our arrangement. Kevin not want any house in St Lawrence Road. The locals won't like it and he want *mend fences?*'

Marku sighed again and stretched out his arms.

'I say him *look at the records*. He see no money passed to me for nine month work.' said Marku, heavily stressing the *'nine'*. He was not happy. He tell me go away and Thames Reach Builders want nothing to do with me.'

'It took five years working sixteen hours a day to raise the money I spent on that house. So I upset - angry. You would be, yes?'

'Thank you, Mr Marku.'

'We'll want to ask you more questions but first we

need to see what Kevin Price has to say. The constable can get you tea and a newspaper while you wait.'

**

Kevin looked impatiently at them as they entered. Kate opened:

'We're sorry about your father's death. We suspect murder and so have to ask everyone where they were on Sunday between 5-7am.'

Ranjit continued:

'We were on our way to ask when we saved you from some nasty bruises. We've talked to Burim Marku but want to hear your side of the story.'

'He came with some cock-and-bull story of owning half the land on which my father built his house. I told him where to go. He grabbed me and shouted in my face so I told him that I wouldn't have need of his services again. You saw what happened next.'

Kate looked him in the eye.

'You'll be surprised when I tell you that Mr Marku's claim is genuine. His solicitor has the deeds. Where can we find the other set of deeds, Mr. Price? Thames Reach Builders' solicitors don't have them.'

Kate thought that while Kevin Price could undoubtedly lie, she doubted that he was a talented actor. In this case, he seemed genuinely shocked.

'In view of that and the murder of your father, we shall need to inspect your accounts. We can get a warrant but it would be easier if you co-operated,' said Ranjit.

Kevin looked none too pleased, but gave his

permission.

'Where were you on Sunday between 5 and 7am, Mr Price?' asked Kate.

'Asleep beside my wife. We didn't get up till almost nine. After a lazy breakfast, I went to play golf. I was on the golf course when Samantha rang me after she'd been to the mortuary. I went straight to her. She was in a bad way.'

'Your father told Samantha that he had to go to the yard. Would anyone have been there at that time on a Sunday morning?' asked Ranjit.

'No, we close the yard from noon on Saturday until 7am on Monday. We've had occasional pilfering so we installed CCTV.'

Thank you, Mr Price. We'll take a look. Make sure all recordings are secure please. Did you find anything that suggests your father went into the office or looked up anything in particular?'

'The news came as shock − more than a shock. I can't believe it even though I've seen his body. That was the last thing I'd think about. Sharon and I haven't said anything to our children. We don't know how to tell them. Peter and Emily loved their granddad. They know that something is up because they've noticed how upset we are. I don't want them to hear it from someone else. Sharon is going to the nursery today to tell them and get some advice.' said Kevin.

'You have our sympathy Mr Price. But, if something does occur to you, here's my phone number,' said Kate handing him her card. Price went to stand up but Ranjit signalled him to stay seated.

'Before I can let you leave - I have to ask some

intrusive questions. I understand that it is difficult at a time like this. But if we are to catch whoever did this to your family, we need as much information as possible,' said Ranjit. 'I need to know about your relationship with your father. What can you tell me?'

Kevin wasn't expecting such an open question.

'What do you want to know?'

'Did you work closely together? Did you see eye to eye about the business?

'… outside of work, did you meet a lot?'

***

They returned to Marku.

'Where were you between 5 and 7am on Sunday?'

'On my boat - asleep. It moored near Iffley on the Thames Reach side of the river.'

'Can anyone verify that?

'No, I only.'

'Then we're finished here for now. You can go, but stay away from Kevin Price. We've told him that your claim is genuine. Maybe you should talk, in a gentle way, with Samantha Price? My advice is, gain her sympathy – keep a lid on that temper of yours. If I hear of any threats or violence, I'll charge you with the assault on Kevin Price. I witnessed it myself.'

***

Ranjit sent Richard Smith with a team to accompany Kevin to examine the financial records at Thames Reach Builders. Marku was dropped off near Iffley Lock. Kate and Ranjit grabbed much needed coffees and went to his office.

'There's no doubt that Marku's on our list of likeliest suspects. He has a somewhat plausible motive and lives on the river not far from where our victim was found, but I'm inclined to believe him. Why should he want to kill Godfrey, when Godfrey had given him joint ownership of the land? Could there be something he isn't telling us?' said Ranjit.

'From what Kevin said, his father didn't share everything with Kevin. In fact, they rarely talked about anything – Kevin wasn't happy about his father's second marriage either. He has a motive and his alibi is his wife. According to Samantha, Godfrey was going to the yard after the phone call. It could've been to meet either of them,' suggested Kate.

They looked at the investigation board. Ranjit moved the images of Kevin and Angela above those of Carol, Samantha and Margaret, designating them as priority investigation targets.

'I'm glad you're seeing Angela tomorrow, Kate.'

He added a photo of Burim Marku after drawing a dividing line between the Price family and others. He'd read the reports of interviews in the Abingdon Way area. The recurring names were George and Carrie Gamble. Their photos were the only other additions to the board. It didn't look at all promising. Some of the team would bet on Burim being the murderer, but he couldn't figure out a strong enough motive. He still couldn't say where the victim was drugged or how the body had arrived where it did. He wasn't looking forward to reporting to the Chief Constable on Friday afternoon. He didn't have so much as a gut feeling. How was he going to show any authority on this, his first big case as a chief inspector? *Maybe I could do with Alex Hornby's fictional detective.*

His mood brightened when PC Jordon came to inform him that there was CCTV footage at Iffley Lock. He'd arranged to get the coverage for last Sunday and to interview the part-time lockkeeper, saying,

'Nowadays, volunteers are needed on the locks and when no lockkeeper is available, the voyagers have to operate the locks by themselves. I'll get the timetables of both Iffley and Sandford Locks and the contact details of all the lockkeepers.' Ranjit nodded his approval, reassured by some measure. He had a good team. So he shouldn't fret. It was early days. But he wished he had an easier case to prove himself to them.

***

'What a difference a week makes!' thought Kevin. The pride and pleasure he'd felt as he parked his car in the large drive in front of their recently bought house backing onto Bagley Woods had dissolved, and now he was overwhelmed by apprehension. How do you talk about death to a four year-old soon to be five, and a three year-old? They adored their granddad. How do you tell them that they'll never see him again – that there will be no granddad at Peter's birthday party? Talking about personal things didn't come naturally to him at the best of times. He didn't want to keep things from Sharon. Now he had another worry.

'What do I tell her about the interrogation at the Police Station?'

Kevin decided the answer was to put it off. He turned the car around and drove back to the office.

CHAPTER 9

BRIXTON

IT HAD BEEN a long time since Kate had visited Brixton. Like Ranjit, she'd worked for a while at the Metropolitan Police. She'd started out as a civilian employee and proved herself in IT research like Richard Smith. She was encouraged to join the CID. Like everyone, she started out as Detective Constable and thought she was prepared for the grind which every newbie had to get through. But after a few years, she realised that it wasn't the institutional intention for her: the guys liked to keep her on grunt duties, such as door-knocking and procuring phone records, rather than accompanying them to crime scenes. They piled computer searches on her as if she were their servant.

That was why she'd moved to Oxfordshire four years ago. She was soon promoted to Detective Sergeant. She was young for the role of CI but that was her ambition. Her age was why she hadn't put her name forward for the post that Ranjit applied for. She aimed to prove herself on this case: it could make a huge difference—make the hierarchy look at her as having potential. When she and Ranjit had been alone together driving to a scene, he was confiding but in a group situation she wasn't convinced that he respected her like he did the guys.

Here she was in old territory. She'd been based in Vauxhall not far from Brixton back in the day. It had been gentrified since then. She'd been a regular customer at the local market and was pleased to discover, before her meeting with Angela, that it was still great for food. Angela's flat was a former council flat, but it was not inside a tower, more like a condominium. Makeovers had obscured their humble origins. Looking around, Kate wondered how a nurse could afford it. She rang the bell. It was opened by a black man with a hairstyle like that of the historian, David Olusoga, who turned out to be his namesake.

'You must be Kate Farr? I'm David, Angela's partner. I hope you don't mind me sitting in?'

Kate shook his hand. David showed her into an elegant lounge. The far end was dominated by a huge psychedelic painting and the wall behind a long sofa was clad in bookcases. On the coffee table were art magazines and a few books. She noticed one by Alex Hornby. David went into the kitchen to fetch Angela.

Kate knew that Angela was twenty-seven, so she was surprised to see that she looked even younger. She was wearing a vintage punk T- shirt over almost delicately ripped jeans. She was tall like her father but her empathetic blue eyes were like her mother's.

Angela saw Kate looking closely at her and stepped forward and gestured her to sit, saying,

'Outside of work, I like to let my hair down –or brighten it up.' she said, combing her fingers through her orange highlights.

'I think we have things in common.' said Kate looking at the copy of *Blood in the Bodleian.* 'I hadn't realised Alex Hornby lives in Thame Reach. Do you know that she found your father's body?'

'Really? Thank you for telling me. Alex lives opposite my grandmother Margaret. She stood out when she first moved to Thames Reach. Almost everyone in the village was white in those days. She seemed exotic. I got to know her when she joined the Amateur Dramatic Society. As well as acting, she offered to write scripts.'

'When was that?' asked Kate.

'Nine years ago, probably. I was doing my A levels then. After I qualified and met this gorgeous guy we decided to move in together. We were visiting my grandmother and I saw Alex in her garden. When I told her that we were struggling to find somewhere we liked, she suggested Brixton. I owe her. She told us about Trinity Gardens. David and I were lucky enough to put a deposit on this flat before prices went sky high. We love it here. It's only a hundred yards from the Tube, it's close to the market and the Roxy but it's quiet. Can I get you a coffee?'

The procedure was to decline, but Kate decided that accepting it could help Angela to relax and become talkative. Her judgement proved right. Kate glanced at the painting while Angela prepared the coffee.

'That's one of mine,' said David. 'I studied at St. Martins and joined a cooperative in Stockwell. Six years ago I had an accident going home and was taken to St Thomas's. Angela nursed me … We bought this place nearly four years ago. We couldn't afford it now, not on artists' and nurses' salaries. I am exhibited but I also work on theatre and film sets...'

He trailed off as Angela returned with the coffee in hand.

'I sympathise with your twelve-hour shifts. They aren't uncommon in the police force either,' said Kate as she took the cup. 'Are you still at St Thomas's?'

'Yes, but I've become an agency worker rather than a staff nurse. It's paid better and it's flexible. It means that I can work over the bank holidays and get a week's pay for it. That way David and I get to see each other more,' replied Angela looking as if she wanted to jump in bed with David and that she had interrupted them. For a moment, Kate envied her. This was a couple in love and in lust.

'I saw you at the reading of your father's will. I'm sorry to intrude, but I noticed that he didn't leave you anything. That must have hurt. A legacy could have helped with your mortgage,' said Kate.

'The hurt happened a long time ago. When Kevin and I were in primary school, Dad could do no wrong. Once we became teenagers, he changed and we noticed things. He was a control freak. My mother was scared of him. Once Kevin grew as tall as Dad, he was a threat to his authority. He expected me to be an obedient little girl and to copy my mother. When I wasn't obsequious, he beat me.'

This was news to Kate. 'I'm sorry. Is that why you moved to London?'

'Yes, I got away as soon as possible. I trained at UCL and things improved. He even bragged about his nurse daughter and rang me for health tips. When a worker was off with something, he'd check it out with me. Kevin went to work for him and towed the line, so Dad seemed quite chuffed as if everything was in its rightful place.' said Angela.

'To be fair, Dad gave me the deposit for this flat. He gave me the money four years ago just after he'd met Samantha. It felt like a bribe to keep me sweet but I was grateful for it. At first Mum wasn't too upset. In some ways her life improved. Then he started to put her down in front of others. She wasn't as reclusive as she is now. She's always been shy, but she enjoyed meeting people. She ran the office efficiently. She was in charge not Mandy. After the divorce, it meant she lost her job, her home, everything. He made her what she is now,' said Angela with a sigh.

'I challenged him about it. I said it was one thing him having a bit on the side but he didn't need to humiliate Mum. She didn't deserve it. She'd been a good wife and done a lot to build his business. People trusted her and she's intelligent. Not like she is now. I expect you've been to Rose Hill?'

'Yes, I was surprised, given how well Thames Reach Builders have done, that she got so little out of the divorce. How did that happen? Was it the bullying behaviour?'

'Oh yes. He said he wouldn't leave the business to Kevin and would write me out of his will entirely, if she complained. *He* bought the flat and moved her into it. I blame myself. We should have got her a good solicitor. Instead, I just didn't go home much and concentrated on my life in London. Kevin was left on his own, on the spot. He's almost six years older than me. It suited him to settle down at twenty-five with Sharon −young for nowadays. Sharon reminds me of how our Mum used to be. She's content to be there for him and the kids. Dad could turn on the charm when he wanted something. He told Kevin that he would raise his salary by £7000 a year and he could look after Mum. He flattered him and said what a *good son* he was, how Mum needed him. Dad's solicitors did the rest. They believed him when he said that Mum was ill and incapable and that this was the best arrangement.'

'Was she ill and incapable?' asked Kate.

'She'd become withdrawn and depressed. In retrospect, it's easy to see that she did need proper help and support. But we can't change the past. I was angry when I realised what had happened. I told Dad that he had cheated Mum, that she deserved half of the business. He pushed me out of the door and slammed it in my face and said he never wanted to see me again. It suited me.'

'What about you and your Mum?' asked Kate.

'I've called on her every month since the divorce.'

'She told me that you stay with an old school friend,' said Kate.

'Yes, Jane lives in Poplar Avenue not far from our old primary school. So I got to see Dad destroy granddad's house and build the fortress for Samantha.'

'I'm sure that you understand that I have to ask you, where you were last weekend,' asked Kate.

'It was my weekend in Oxfordshire. I visited Mum on Saturday and coaxed her out and drove her to Shotover Hill for a walk. It was a pleasant day and she let me take her to the King's Arms for lunch. I thought she looked better for it. There was a little colour in her cheeks. She told me that she's started writing poetry. I suggested she join a group but that was too much too soon. She needs help but it's hard getting it. I see it every day. The NHS is chronically short of staff and none more so than the mental health services. I don't have the means to pay for private counselling but I suggested to Kevin that he could afford it.'

'What did Kevin say?'

'That he'd think about it but things were tight for him. He moved house six months ago and has taken on a big mortgage. His wife wants their two kids to go to private schools so they need to save. The £7000 for mum didn't leave anything after paying the community charge, telephone, energy and her food.'

'So you stayed overnight with Jane?

'Not exactly. I stayed at Jane's as usual but she wasn't there.

She was on a city break to Barcelona. We reciprocate. She likes staying here when she comes to London.'

'Then you have no-one to confirm that you were at Poplar Avenue between 5 and 7am?'

'That's right. I disapprove of how my father behaved towards Mum and me but that doesn't mean that I hate him enough to commit murder. He's my father, and once upon a time he even behaved like one. I wouldn't kill him. I'm a nurse for god's sake! I've spent my life healing not injuring and I'm aunt to Peter and Emily. They just adored their grandfather. He's to them more like the dad we knew at their age.'

'Did David come with you to Oxford?'

'No, and he has an alibi that can be confirmed. He was in Liverpool where he has an exhibition.'

***

Kate arrived back in Kidlington at 6pm. Ranjit was still at the station and not looking happy. Kate sat down to type up her report and informed him while he leaned against a wall.

'I liked her but the facts look suspicious. She was in Thames Reach on Saturday night and has no one to confirm her whereabouts between 5 and 7am. Poplar Avenue is only half a mile from the industrial estate. There's a footpath leading to it running next to the cemetery. As an intensive care nurse she has access to insulin. She has enough reason to resent her father, but ...

'She doesn't strike you as someone who'd want revenge?' said Ranjit. 'Not another one!'

'But, if we're wrong and she resented him more than she wants us to know, then she'd have the means and could be in the right place at the right time to do it. Any news at your end?'

'The report from the Thames expert came in. If the body was dropped off a boat anywhere in the middle of river a mile beyond Sandford, it could have ended up where it did,' said Ranjit.

'So we're looking for boats?'

'Good luck there. None were spotted on the CCTV going through Iffley lock on Sunday morning before eight. There were a couple around 8.30am but by the time they reached Sandford, it would've been too late. There's no CCTV at Sandford Lock. Whoever did this chose a pretty useful place to dispose of a body.'

Ranjit prepared to report to Chief Constable Rayner. She looked friendly enough as he went in.

'Bring me up to date.' she said indicating that he should sit.

'I wish I had good news to report, Ma'am. We are treating it as murder but it's unusual. Normally there are some clues at the scene of the crime. In this case, we don't know the scene of the crime. Any DNA had been washed away and we have no idea how the body got where it was found. For the moment, we're assuming that it was dropped off a boat.'

She seemed sympathetic until Ranjit asked for the weekend off.

'Two months ago, I booked this weekend off for my cousin's wedding in Birmingham, Ma'am. I'd like to leave DS Farr in charge.'

'You don't need me to tell you how CRUCIAL the first ten days are in an investigation like this. I'm disappointed in you, Chief Inspector. This is your first big case in the limelight. Thames Reach Builders is a well- known Oxfordshire firm with good contacts in the County Council. We'll be under pressure to produce answers soon and you think a cousin's wedding more important?'

Ranjit was not looking forward to telling Jia.

***

'I don't ask much of you, Ranjit. We came here to support you, but I miss my London colleagues and the twins hated leaving their friends. You need to spend time with them. Didn't you even try to explain how important weddings are to families like ours?'

Seeing Ranjit's expression of regret, Jia relented.

'I expect that, to her, family means four or five people not a hundred like they do for us. I bet she's never even met her cousins, let alone her second cousins and their partners and children.'

CHAPTER 10

RABBIT WARRENS

ALEX WAS NOT prone to superstition. Yet, she couldn't stop picturing the aftermath of the guided walk which she had given Jo and Cleo. This weekend she walked alone. She'd made her usual start along Sustrans but diverted to Reach Meadows by the rabbit warren, hoping to see a water vole in the stream. It had rained well so there was a chance. She had her usual coffee at Proof Social where all the chat was about the happenings at their neighbouring business. The ethos of the Tap Social organisation was that at least twenty five percent of staff should be ex- offenders. They weren't surprised to get a visit from the police given their proximity to Thames Reach Builders. There were a few comments doing the rounds like,

'They're having problems finding who did it. Make sure you have your alibi ready in case they want to make us oven-ready scapegoats.'

Alex joked in return, but also answered it seriously in case some of them were genuinely worried.

'I found the body so I've seen a lot of the investigating team. You haven't anything to worry about.'

She finished her Danish pastry and set off on a marked path around a new development and headed towards Radley College. After walking through the college grounds, she headed for the woods, following a green signed way across the field. Samantha had told her that Godfrey owned it, but it struck Alex as strange that in his will, half had been given to her grumpy neighbour, Frank Foreman, of all people.

Most of it was ploughed but all four corners had precious hazel and aspen coppice. She wasn't surprised to come across George and Carrie Gamble taking photographs. She stopped and enquired what they were looking at.

'These are Herb Paris and those green flower orchids are quite rare. This area is important for wood white butterflies. They became almost extinct in Oxfordshire but are returning.'

Carrie pointed to the coppice close to Radley Woods.

'A rare Cetti's Warbler has nested there.'

'Any particular reason for the photographs?' asked Alex.

'Councillor Frank Foreman has applied for planning permission to build fifty houses on this field.'

'What? When did he do that?' asked Alex. 'I thought he was in Australia.'

'He's back. Look, that's him over there walking with Kevin Price.'

Alex rang Kate and suggested they meet for coffee at the King's Arms. She had something to report which could be of interest. It was Kate's only day off, but she agreed.

'I'm off duty so we could have lunch if you like. It's on me as I appreciate your contribution,' said Kate.

The weather was dry and warm, so they sat outside overlooking Sandford Lock. Kate raised a glass, 'Here's to your next book. What's it about, by the way? Have you a title?'

'*Bad Blood in Summertown*. It's a hidden mafia

story. As you are one of my readers, I won't tell you anymore and spoil the fun.'

'I interviewed Angela Price on Friday. She said you used to live in Brixton. What made you come here?'

'I came after my divorce with my ex-husband, Andrew. We had to sell the house in Trinity Gardens and divide the proceeds. I couldn't afford to buy in London so looked in Oxford. I knew a little of the area – I'd been on local courses and Andrew had studied here as a medical student. He used to enjoy showing me where he'd sowed his 'wild oats'.'

Kate heard a click but wasn't sure where the noise came from but continued focusing on Alex's words.

'I knew I'd like it but I discovered that I couldn't afford to buy in Oxford either. It's still the case now. I'm lucky to have enough revenue from my books to live on, if I supplement it with some teaching and freelance writing, but unless they're turned into films or TV series, it will remain tight to live in Oxfordshire. I could only just afford to buy my house in Thames Reach.'

'It looks like we've made a similar journey. I lived in Vauxhall. My partner and I started to grow apart and my career was going nowhere fast. Oxfordshire appointed a female Chief Constable and I thought that a good sign.'

Alex raised her glass and hesitated a little before she asked,

'How do you find working with your boss? You don't have to answer but I hope you don't mind this crime writer being curious?'

'Can I trust you to tell no one else?

Alex nodded.

'Being black, you'll have an idea of the kind of problems he faced in the MET. I've noticed that non-white men can be on the receiving end of racist banter but act in the same way as some white colleagues when it comes to women. Ranjit takes my ability for granted without recognising it.'

'Can you give me an example?'

'He enjoys a joke at our expense. He's noticed that you and I have connected well and uses it to undermine me. I expect he thinks it's funny but it doesn't feel quite so amusing on the receiving end. The reason I left the MET was to get away from the banter. If you didn't laugh at it, you were regarded as being a *sour cow* with no sense of humour.'

'Why not try giving as good as you get?'

'Is that what you've learned?'

'My mother's best friend was a nurse of the Windrush generation. She didn't want to count the number of times she was told by patients to "*take your dirty black hands off me.*" Because I'm not treated like that, I tend to let the minor things wash over me.'

'Maybe I should copy you. Its early days,' said Kate and then changed the subject. 'I'm still renting but I'm hoping to buy somewhere soon.'

Alex guessed what she was thinking.

'The good thing about Thames Reach is having a reasonable sized garden. It suits the writer's life. I can't write nonstop all day. And we're spoilt for choice when it comes to walks. I made a good choice. That's why I'm still here after twelve years.'

Remembering how she used chance encounters

to drive plots, Alex decided to tell Kate about what she'd seen and heard about the field near the college.

'I hope you don't mind if I flag it up on social media. We need to stop this development. I agree with George and Carrie, we can't just put a stop to further destruction of the natural world, we do have to start regenerating it. I wouldn't put it past Frank to spray it with Round Up and destroy the diversity before it even gets to the planning committee. The village needs to protect it in the meantime. George has infrared night cameras. I think we should install them there.'

Kate made a noncommittal hum. There was something else on her mind.

***

After the meal, they walked slowly across the wooden bridge to the side of the lock. The volunteer lockkeeper had closed the gates and was lowering the water level. The Salter's steamer filled the lock. They looked down at the people on the deck. The lockkeeper walked to the Abingdon side and slowly opened the gates. The steamer glided out gracefully.

Once the gates were closed, Kate and Alex walked over them and, for a moment, Alex looked downstream. The current was fast-flowing. A flash of an idea crossed her mind. She glanced at Kate and could see that her grey cells were spinning.

'Let's talk to the lockkeeper.'

They introduced themselves to him. John was a volunteer lockkeeper. Kate asked if he'd been on duty on the previous Sunday. He hadn't, but he gave them the name of the volunteer who was on duty that day from 10am to 4pm.

'What would happen if the lock was full or almost full and you opened the gates?' asked Alex.

'You can't open the tail gates when the lock is full but, from time to time, a log drifts downstream into the lock. If it's small we pull it out, but if it's large and that isn't practical or safe, we flush it downstream. To do that you almost empty the lock, then we open the tail gates. By opening the head gate sluices we can send a flow of water downstream and flush the log out.'

Kate looked thoughtful and saw that Alex was of the same mind. They wondered what would happen if someone were to open the sluices with a body in the lock?

Kate asked John,

'What about a body?' If you opened the sluice gates as much as possible, what would be the effect?'

'The force of the water would be powerful. I wouldn't want to be moored at the Abingdon side at the moment the water gushed out, the body would be moving fast,' said John.

'So if anything was in the lock it would be swept away?' asked Kate.

'Oh yes, and a long way too,' said John.

CHAPTER 11

HOW DUNNIT

KATE WAS EXCITED when she told the team her findings at Sandford Lock.

'No-one would've been around at 6am aside from a possible jogger or dog walker. We need to put out an appeal for information. Anyone using the Thames regularly for leisure would know how to operate the locks. If someone had access to the key for the gates at the end of Sandford Lane, they could even drive a car in from the Thames Reach side. If that person threw in the body, opened the tail gates towards Abingdon and then opened the sluices, a strong current could take the body more than a mile downstream.'

There was a murmur around the room. It seemed like a plausible location for the scene of the crime. But a week had already passed. Would any evidence remain? Ranjit asked the team working on Thames Reach Builders if they had a key for the gate at the end of the road, or if anyone else on the industrial estate had access to one.

Kate had more to report: the news about the proposed new development near the college and Councillor Frank Foreman's involvement.

'He's been in Australia but Alex was surprised to see him back, he wasn't expected till next week. I think we should check if he was in the country on the weekend of the murder. Can someone get immigration details of flights from Australia that week?'

It didn't take long to confirm that Frank had arrived at Heathrow on Friday May 22, two days before the murder. Where had he stayed if not his home? Could he have stayed with Kevin?'

Ranjit added the name Frank Foreman to the board.

'Sir, Alex also made a comment that could be of interest.'

Ranjit struggled to stop himself making a sarcastic remark.

'She says that Frank complains a lot about being hard up and how expensive it is running a car, but his trip to Australia was not on the cheap. No expense was spared.'

At last, Ranjit felt that they could be getting somewhere and acknowledged Kate's good work with this and with Angela. He'd needed that blast of confidence after the difficult conversation with the Chief Constable. The burden of responsibility felt heavy and he needed his sergeant so should perhaps show it?

***

Ranjit was examining the ownership of the land in Abingdon Way and Radley Fields when the phone rang. It was Peter Jordan calling from Thames Reach Builders. 'Sir, I've looked at the CCTV footage on the morning of the murder. There was a break-in at 5.50 am. I recognised the woman. You couldn't fail to.'

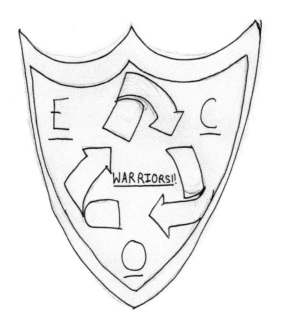

CHAPTER 12

ECO WARRIORS

IT DIDN'T TAKE long to pick up George and Carrie Gamble. Kate took a long look through the one-way glass, curious to see how Carrie reacted to waiting alone. She appeared calm. She was wearing green chinos, a baggy black sweater and Doc Martins. Her long chestnut hair was loose. No jewellery. She was smaller than she looked in the photo on the board - maybe 5 feet 4? They interviewed her first.

'Are you a full-time activist?' asked Ranjit.

'No, I'm studying at Brookes – environmental studies.'

'Why did you break into Thames Reach Builders on Sunday 24th May?'

'So you know? How?'

Kate turned the laptop around and played the CCTV. It was clear that George had held a ladder to the gate and Carrie had jumped into the yard. It was only when she walked to the warehouse that you could clearly see Carrie's face.

'It took us time to discover this. The yard hadn't even bothered to check their recordings – they weren't aware of the break-in, due to nothing appearing to have been stolen. We found it because we're investigating the murder of Godfrey Price who was probably killed at around the time of this video.'

'That was nothing to do with me. Look, you took my iPhone. If you let me have it back, I'll show you why I was there.'

A few minutes later PC Chen entered with the phone. Under Ranjit's watchful eye, Carrie brought up images of large drums of Glyphosate weed killer that she had photographed in the corner of the warehouse.

'I was told by a friend that they were stocking this. Godfrey used it to kill almost everything that was growing at number 1 Abingdon Way. Then he smothered the ground with decking and paving. Granddad and I heard rumours that they want to do the same on Radley Fields- eradicate plant life.'

'So why not just go there when it was open, if you just wanted to take pictures?' asked Ranjit.

'They know me and Granddad. They see us as **terrorists** because we tried to stop them cutting down the oaks. We held the destruction up for months and they had to go to court,' said Carrie proudly. 'They would never let me rummage around. These were covered with tarpaulin and hidden behind a stack of plasterboard.'

'Why are you so concerned about them having Glyphosate? That's Round Up isn't it? asked Ranjit.

'*Round Up* is evil. It kills almost everything and gets deep into the soil, damaging biodiversity. Can I show you some research from McGill University in Montreal?'

Ranjit nodded and let Kate bring up the paper Carrie wanted them to see.

"We observed significant loss of biodiversity in communities contaminated with glyphosate. This could have a profound impact on the proper functioning of ecosystems by lowering their chance

of adapting to new pollutants or stressors. This is particularly concerning as many ecosystems are grappling with the increasing threat of pollution and climate change." Carrie continued,

'Godfrey Price and Frank Foreman would destroy all the wild flowers with this if they have their way. To them they are pernicious weeds. I tried talking to them. I asked them to think about the future of life on earth. It depends on the quality of the air we breathe, the water we drink and the soil we grow our food in and glyphosate damages soil for years and loss of wild flowers leads to a decline in pollinators. But they didn't listen. They call me 'that IDIOT girl'.'

'So you broke in to prove they have it,' finished Kate.

'Yes.'

'That seems drastic.'

'Price and Foreman want to build on Radley Fields. We might not be able to prevent that completely, though where future residents will access a doctor, I've no idea. At the very least, we must stop them destroying the hedgerows and coppices on the site. A responsible builder would see them as an asset but not those two. A rare Cetti's Warbler is nesting in this hazel.'

Carrie brought up a picture.

'These are rare plants for this area,' she said, pointing to their photos of Herb Paris and green orchids. 'If they use Glyphosate it will destroy them and the insects that are part of the ecology. We have to stop them.'

'How long were you in the yard, and what and who

did you see?'

'Granddad parked behind Proof Social and we took the ladders to the rear of yard. As I was crossing it to get out, I looked back towards the office. I can't swear that someone was in there −I heard something fall over and ran.'

George's story matched Carrie's. Ranjit had no reason to think that they were lying. It was what they cared about.

'Aren't you worried that you are encouraging your granddaughter to break the law? A criminal record won't help her future.'

'The law is man-made. There was a time when it was legal to buy and sell human beings. There was a time when the law gave a man ownership of his wife's body and all her possessions upon marriage. Nature is more important than the law. If we destroy the environment, there will be no future for mankind. Our laws will become irrelevant.'

Given what she'd heard about George, Kate wondered if that was the biggest speech he'd ever made.

'I'm proud of Carrie. I can't tell you how proud I am of her.'

'I could charge you with breaking and entering. I should but I won't. Thames Reach Builders will want me to, but it won't be wise of them to push too hard. I can't promise to react in the same way if you trespass there again.'

***

'Do you think it worth looking for evidence of insulin in the office?' asked Kate.

'Let's send Veronica Chen with a forensic specialist to give it a thorough examination.'

Arriving at the yard, they showed their search warrant to Mandy and asked her to leave the premises.

'Can I at least take the computer so I can do some work?' she asked.

'We'll start with your desk, so it won't be long before we can give it to you.'

After receiving a call from Chen, Ranjit and Kate set out for the Sandford Lane site. As they approached the door to the office, a furious Kevin Price hurried towards them his eyes glaring but with a hint of despair in his expression.

'I've tried to be helpful but this is too much. Have you any idea how many people's incomes these stoppages effect? I'm a decent boss and want to pay my employees even when they can't work. What about the subcontractors? If we lose the goodwill of customers because we don't respond to their emails and calls, I can't give them work either. Some delays are unavoidable due to the weather, but this? How many visits do you need to make before we can be left to get on with earning a living? '

Ranjit looked equally annoyed.

'I too have a job to do, SIR. I'm surprised that I need to remind you that we are investigating your father's murder.'

Veronica Chen took Ranjit aside and whispered,

'We've found traces of insulin and there are insulin pens in the secretary's desk and a bag full of insulin files. It looks like it's on prescription. Let me show you.'

***

'If you'd told us what you were looking for, we could have avoided all this disruption,' said Mandy Smith. 'I've type one Diabetes.'

Ranjit tried to look sympathetic hoping she would co-operate.

'I'm sorry about that, but doing our job often causes some inconvenience. We'd like to ask you some questions and then we'll leave you in peace,' said Ranjit. 'Do you always keep the insulin in that drawer?'

'Yes, I do.'

'Has any gone missing in recent weeks?'

'I wouldn't know, I don't always keep count. My life is busy - busy enough as it is with work and family.' Why would anyone want to take my insulin? '

Ranjit looked at her as if she was living in different world to him.

'If you need to inject, where do you do it?'

Mandy pointed to a door.

'In the shower room. We had that installed two years ago. If the men have been on a particularly dirty job, they appreciate showering and changing before getting into their own vehicles. We look after our workers. That's why they're loyal to us.'

'So you've never injected by that filing cabinet?' asked Kate.

'No.'

'That's helpful, Mrs Smith. We'll need to talk to you about the business, about any complaints or any disgruntled clients. It's routine. We have to be able to exclude some lines of investigation. Can you suggest a time later this week when Kate and I can come and talk to you and Kevin?'

They settled on Friday. Ranjit hoped that Richard Smith would be able to tell him more about the company and give him some possible leads before then.

'At least we're getting a clearer picture of '*how*'. There are two possible sources of insulin, Nurse Angela Price and Mandy Smith who has a prescription. There are people who will know that Mandy has some in the office. Given that traces of insulin were found on the filing cabinet and indications that a body had leant against it, we can assume that the office of Thames Reach Builders is the initial scene of the crime. If Carrie Gamble is correct and she heard something fall in the office, the time of the crime is probably 6.10 am. The injury to the head could have been caused then and not on the rock in the riverbank. The body could have been transported to Sandford Lock at the end of the lane.'

'We've asked forensics to investigate car tracks, particularly any beyond the padlocked gate. We've had heavy rain so we'll be lucky to find anything but it's worth a try. Thames Reach Builders don't have a key to that gate but the lockkeepers and the volunteers all have keys, so getting a copy of it wouldn't be too challenging. Now we need to concentrate on WHO did it, and on that we aren't much closer.'

'All the suspects have a motive to wish ill on Godfrey Price, but a motive worth killing for?' said Ranjit pointing to the board.

'There are still two on there who we haven't interviewed, Frank Foreman and Margaret Pugh,' said Kate.

'I want to interview Frank Foreman, but we need more on him before we do. Peter, take a look at council records. How long has he been a councillor, the planning issues he's dealt with, etc. And Kate, you can interview Margaret Pugh.'

Ranjit tried hard to look confident. They were making progress but, every time he looked in the mirror he became uneasy. Do I look like a Chief Inspector?

CHAPTER 13

DIGGING DEEP

IT EXPERT RICHARD and Peter Jordan sat opposite Ranjit in his office.

'Frank Foreman pleads poverty and lives modestly in Thames Reach in a semi-detached house in Woodland Road. Surprising then that when he's in London or Bournemouth, he stays in the best rooms in the best hotels. He has the best seats whenever he goes to watch Manchester United. He flew first class to Australia, stopping at Singapore on the way where he stayed in Raffles.'

'Sounds like he leads a double life. What can you tell me about his council record?'

'He was a Parish Councillor for ten years and then was elected to the District Council eight years ago. For the past four years he's been chair of the Planning Committee. His lavish shadow life started two years ago,' said Peter.

'We know he was friendly with Godfrey and shares ownership of Radley Fields with Kevin. Is there anything else that links them?'

'Frank's son, the one in Australia, is the same age as Kevin. They went to school together and were close friends. James Foreman worked for Thames Reach builders until three years ago. He went to live in Perth where he's set up a business building swimming pools.'

'Let's take a look at Councillor Foreman's bank

accounts before we invite him for tea, shall we?'

***

Margaret Pugh's house was opposite Frank Foreman's. Kate noticed his modest Ford Focus parked in his totally paved-over front garden. It took a long time for Margaret to open the door.

When she eventually did, the woman facing Kate hardly looked older than her daughter Carol. For someone with dementia, she was the opposite of frail. Her body appeared remarkably fit and strong but then it was the mind most affected. Kate followed her into the lounge and noticed her jumper was on inside out. Margaret turned off the television.

'I'm sorry to bother you. I'm sure you've heard about the death of Godfrey Price?' said Kate.

'Yes. Angela told me.'

'Do you see Angela often?'

'She's a good girl.'

'We believe Godfrey was murdered on Sunday May 14 between 6.30 and 7 am. We have to ask people who knew him well what they were doing at that time. Where were you then, Mrs Pugh?'

'I can't remember.'

'Your near neighbour, Alex, said she found you sitting on a bench in the children's playground looking lost and confused at 6.30 pm on Sunday. Do you remember where you'd been, Mrs Pugh?'

Margaret became agitated, looked distressed and her right hand trembled.

'I'm sorry that I have to ask these questions. Can I

get you a cup of tea?'

Margaret nodded. Kate used the chance to look at the kitchen. It was uncluttered compared to Carol's but she noticed a gas burner was on with nothing on it on the hob. She switched off the gas and switched on the electric kettle. When she returned with the tea, Margaret was pacing up and down the room. She led her back to her chair and handed her the tea.

'Do you see your grandson Kevin much?'

Margaret shook her head and her eyes glazed over as if she was somewhere else.

'What about Godfrey? Living in the same village, you must've seen him out and about a lot.'

Margaret muttered something, but Kate couldn't help notice a steely flash in her eyes.

'Do you know Frank Foreman?' asked Kate anticipated a simple answer of 'yes'. What she heard shed an unexpected new light.

CHAPTER 14

KAYAKING

THE DAY WAS warm, the sun shone and Robbie and Khai succumbed to temptation. For the first time in their young lives, they bunked school. They left to catch the school bus outside Thames Reach Post Office but after a hundred yards, turned back and crept into Robbie's garden shed to change into shorts and T-shirts and, most importantly, collect their fishing gear.

Approaching Sandford Lock, they left the Thames Path and took an overgrown path to their private spot to set up camp. Shielded by a willow they began to unpack, when Robbie pointed to the still pool beneath the weir where an upturned Kayak was floating.

'It's our lucky day,' said Khai. 'How do we reach it?'

'How about I swim out and pull it back?'

Robbie did just that and Khai helped him right the boat. As it turned, it revealed the body of a drowned man. From that day, Robbie and Khai could not see the Thames Reach football club tie without the horror of their discovery etched in sunlit brilliance.

***

Kate looked at the body. With those distinctive protruding upper teeth, there was no denying this was the body of Frank Foreman.

'He won't be answering many questions now, Sir.'

'But we'll probably find more honest answers.'

***

Two days later, the team stood in front of an extended investigation board. Pinpointed on the map was the location where the boys had found the body of Frank Foreman.

Ranjit opened:

'Foreman was dead before he went in the water. A blow to the back of his head was the cause of death. The pathologist's report suggests he fell backwards and hit his head on something metal. Despite being in the water, there was a trace left in his skull.'

'He was found under a Kayak. Any luck finding who owned it?'

'There are a lot of boathouses - college, town and sea scouts between Oxford and Iffley. We asked them all yesterday. None of them reported a missing kayak. There was no-one around when we called at the Sea Scouts so I'm planning to try again this evening when it will definitely be open.

'It may be worth ringing Radley College even though it's in the other direction,' said PC Chen.

'What about CCTV?'

'Unfortunately, the Iffley Lock CCTV only covers the lock itself. A kayak wouldn't need to use the lock. It could use the slipway next to the Thames Path.'

Ranjit nodded agreement. He also thought that he should talk to Veronica Chen to see if she was interested in joining the CID. She noticed things.

'The most likely scenario is that the boat came off the Thames at the weir, turned over in the rapids and floated one hundred yards to the still water in the cut where the boys found him. It's estimated that Foreman died between 11pm and midnight, the day before they found his body. From his diary, he had a meeting pencilled in for a meal with "the boys" at The Tree in Iffley at 8.30 pm.' Ranjit nodded towards Kate.

'We were interested in questioning him about his business dealings with Godfrey Price and whether bribery and corruption in planning were involved. If it was, we are no closer to finding evidence of it.'

Richard Smith looked triumphant and waved some papers near Ranjit's face.

'Sir, I've looked at his bank accounts. His change of behaviour spending on hotels and expensive meals can be accounted for by the £300,000 life insurance that came to him on the death of his wife three years ago.'

'I suppose I should thank you Richard but it's not exactly good news for our investigation. While that doesn't rule out cash payments for favours, it could mean that our suspicions are misplaced. Kate, tell us what we know about the victim.'

'Frank was born in and grew up in Thames Reach. He would've known Godfrey most of his life although at sixty-seven, he was eight years older than him. Frank was an insurance salesman. That could explain the big life insurance on his wife - a perk of his job?

'Not long after his wife's death, his only son James emigrated to Perth in Western Australia. Frank had just returned from visiting him and his partner. We've spoken to James. He's getting a flight to Heathrow tomorrow. Frank's only other living relations are Margaret Pugh and her family. Margaret's maiden name was Foreman and the Edwardian house that she is living in was their childhood home.'

Ranjit looked surprised.

'There doesn't appear to be any love lost between brother and sister. Until recently she was an outspoken critic of his politics. Her sympathies lie with the Gambles. She's known in the village for describing her brother, Godfrey and their mates as the 'Blokey Bullies'. Can you tell us any more about that, DI Farr?'

'Frank was well known for his 'banter' of the type that women find hard to deal with. There was a comic element to them. Women, I've spoken to, say that it's hard to respond the way they'd like without looking like killjoys with no sense of humour. As you gather from 'Blokey Bullies', Margaret was the exception who seemed able to give them as good as she got.' Kate paused for a minute and looking straight at Ranjit said,

'Maybe some of us can learn from her. But then, she did have the advantage of being eleven years older than Frank. As his big sister, I expect she would have been in charge of him when he was a child. But, in general, women around them don't contradict him. How unusual is that?'

Ranjit looked annoyed.

'Detective Sergeant I suggest you stick the point. Time is not on our side, so don't waste it.'

'I've spoken to James Foreman on the phone. He's confirmed the circumstances of her death. He told me that he had blamed his father for the death of his mother, but now believes he was wrong.'

'What's that all about?' asked Ranjit.

'Julie's optician discovered early signs of glaucoma, so she was referred to the Eye Hospital at the John Radcliffe. The tests involve the use of drops that lead to blurring for a few hours, so patients are told not to drive. The arrangement was that Julie was going to call Frank to collect her at the end of her appointment. She'd called on his mobile to collect her but it was switched off. Julie had a work colleague who lived in Saxon Way, almost opposite the rear entrance to the hospital. She rang her friend who suggested she come for tea and that if Frank didn't answer after that, she would drive her home.'

'Hurry it up if you can. I don't have Alex Hornby's luxury of plenty of thinking time and inventing the culprit.'

Kate felt her face redden.

'I'll try to, Sir, without missing out anything important.'

Kate felt bruised in front of her colleagues.

'It was mid-December and at 4.30pm it was already dark. Julie exited the hospital drive onto Saxon Way. There were no cars coming, so she started to cross the road. The drops had blurred her vision and she failed to see the cyclist coming at speed down the hill. He had no means of avoiding her because she walked straight into his path. The collision resulted in her being knocked over and hitting her head with some force on the kerb. She died in intensive care two days later. The injury to Frank is not so dissimilar.'

'That's why James blamed his father for the death of his mother. He knew she was frightened of losing her sight and James thought Frank should have gone with her to the appointment. He was emotional on the phone. He felt grateful that Frank had visited him in Perth and their relationship had improved.' added Peter Jordan.

Ranjit stood up.

'Thank you both. We're getting a better idea of the characters of both Godfrey and Frank but are no closer to finding their killer. In the meantime, we'll treat them as related with the same perpetrator. This "boys' meal" at The Tree is worth investigating. Go to the pub, Peter and find out if it's a regular event, how many of them there were and names if they know them. Kate, talk to Samantha and see if she knows anything about this boys' group.'

'Peter and Veronica, search Thames Valley Builders again to see if there is evidence of a struggle having taken place there.'

Ranjit was about to distribute more tasks when Chief Constable Rayner entered.

'We need to talk, *now*' - with a strong emphasis on 'now'.

***

'The Chairman of the Parish Council, the District Councillor and the County Councillor have been here as a delegation from Thames Reach. They say that the village can cope with one murder, but two in two weeks is too much. They've been bombarded by anxious villagers. The parents at the school gates are talking of nothing else. Some of Frank's friends are making wild accusations against Burim Marku threatening to beat him up if they see him. They demand a meeting.'

'I wish I knew what to say that could mollify them, Ma'am.'

As Ranjit left the building to go home, he was surrounded by clicking cameras and microphones. Two bodies in the Thames near Thames Reach in two weeks had become national news. He and the Chief Constable had agreed that they would call a meeting of the press to which the Thames Reach Councillors would be invited.

'I can confirm that we are treating the death of Councillor Foreman as suspicious. We'll organise a press conference in two days' time. Thank you.'

He pushed his way through the crowd.

***

Ranjit arrived home exhausted, hoping to have one of Jia's mouth- watering South Indian *thalis* and crash out on the sofa to watch a soccer match. It wasn't to be. Home felt as oppressive as the hassle outside the station.

'You're all over the news, Da. It's so embarrassing having a father as a policeman,' said Roshan.

'Where's your sister?'

'How should I know? She stormed out - said she

was going to the library for some peace and quiet. She doesn't like my music.'

Jia came downstairs and gave Roshan a hug.

'You can handle it. Your father's a detective not a policeman on the beat. Pretend he's Alex Hornby's Inspector Parker. He's a pretty cool character and because she's black your friends will relate to that, too.'

'I haven't got any friends. They are all in London.'

Jia tried to give her son a hug but he shook her off. Ranjit looked at his wife with empathy but he understood his son. He'd been there and done that. As a teenage boy he'd felt the same way about his mother's embrace - embarrassed. Jia tried again but with words of advice.

'It's hard when you uproot. I get it. Everyone else knows each other. Look for mates who are new like you. You'll find some. Those refugee kids from Afghanistan must need friends. Why don't you try them?'

Roshan grunted, picked up his iPad and went to his room. Jia kissed Ranjit.

'You look like you can do with a cup of tea or something stronger?'

'Tea will be fine. I'm not sure all this limelight is for me. I want to crawl under a stone and hide.'

'At least, on Saturday, you can relax and unwind at your parents. Have some normal family life. Roshan and Amber are looking forward to it. Their cousins from New York will be there. They really bonded at the wedding.'

A flicker of despair spread across his face.

'I can't go with you. Two deaths and they are expecting me to have the answer yesterday. Ask Amber to explain to Nana-ji? He'll take it from her.'

Jia's empathy wavered.

'I went to the wedding alone and that was bad enough. Niraj and Sushma have to go back to the States on Tuesday. If you don't come on Saturday, you'll miss them altogether. That's so rude.'

'You're right, but what can I do? These aren't normal circumstances, not that anything is ever normal in the CID. I'm not normal, either. I'm the only Sikh Chief Inspector. I can't fail, Jia. I mustn't fail.'

'When I married you, I thought I'd see more of you than friends who married doctors. How wrong was I? I've been working out my notice period, working from home but, have you forgotten that my new job at Brookes starts next month and then I'll need you to help a bit with the twins. They need you, Ranji.'

***

The reporter from the Daily Mail noticed that crime writer Alex Hornby had found the first body. There must be a story in that somewhere. He asked the paper to find her address for him from the electoral register. He headed for Thames Reach and rang the bell of her house in Woodland Road, but there was no answer. Successful journalism involved lots of hanging around so he found a chair in the garden and waited.

CHAPTER 15

SORRY I HAVEN'T A CLUE.

IT WAS A mark of her newfound friendship with Cleo and Alex that Samantha asked them to call her Sam.

'I've never liked the name Samantha. Mum said my dad chose it because he liked someone with that name on a radio programme, *I'm Sorry I Haven't a Clue*. Two years ago, I listened to an episode. But Samantha said not a word. She was there to be the butt of sexy jokes. I guess the imaginary Samantha looked like me. Since then I've preferred to call myself Sam.'

'What do you think of Cleo's idea, Alex?' asked Sam.

'It's a brilliant idea for both of you.'

The suggestion was to use the swimming pool, gym and conservatory as the location for a fitness business – the conservatory being for Pilates and yoga.

'First thing in the morning and after eight in the evening, they could be reserved for the Air B&B tenants,' said Sam, 'but from ten in the morning till seven pm, it would be for Personalised Fitness.'

Alex stared at her. *Had she forgotten that she's pregnant?*

'I don't think you realise how much that tiny little being will turn your life upside down. You may need to develop the business gradually. What could help was if your home and the Air BnB are separate. This space is huge. It would still be large if you cut off that corner to turn into a compact kitchen/diner and playroom with an extra staircase to the two bedrooms above it. That would make your living space separate, and the conservatory could be your lounge. You could let the rest of the house and it would still include three double en–suite bedrooms and one single room. Once it's divided, you could easily let it to visiting professors for six months at a time.'

'Where would I get the money to do the work?

'You need to meet the Albanian builder. I've made some enquiries and I don't think he's a bad guy. To get the freehold back on the land, at least the bit your house is built on, in return you could give him the land at the bottom of the garden. Maybe you can come to some arrangement? Then your bank will give you a mortgage.'

'I asked Kevin how I could contact this Marku, and he swore to have no idea where he lives. I don't believe him but what can I do?'

'Your solicitor can contact him. Say that you would like to see if you can settle the situation in an amicable way.' Sam was on the phone to Challenor and Jones when the intercom buzzed. It was Kate. She was surprised to find Cleo and Alex.

'I need to ask you a few questions related to Godfrey.' She looked towards Alex and Cleo, in a manner that suggested they should leave.

'It's okay' said Sam, 'Cleo and Alex are my lifeline. I keep waking up at night wondering who'd want to kill Goldie. Thinking about it twenty four hours a day would be poisonous for the baby and it's urgent that I get an income if Goldie's child is to have a secure future. I couldn't get my head around it let alone do anything, without them.'

Sam looked at Cleo and Alex through grateful tears.

'I don't want any secrets from them. Let them stay, please.'

Kate nodded in agreement.

'Would you mind telling me how you and Godfrey met?'

'I told you that I worked for Boots but I supplemented my income by working two evenings a week at the Roof Top Club. Do you know it?'

'No, where is that?'

'It's a private men's club over the top of Clarence Bank in the High Street. It has wonderful views of Christchurch and gives the appearance of respectability. It has a library and a lounge but most of the action takes place around the bar. There are dining tables, but the food is provided by the Fusion Asian restaurant next door. Membership is reserved for men but there are women there. They call themselves escorts. There were private rooms on the second floor. I worked as a waitress - yes – really!'

'I fetched food orders from next door. I didn't have to go outside – there was a linking door in the basement between 121 and 123 which opened into the restaurant kitchen.'

'Godfrey was a member. When my Mum died, he noticed how sad I looked. I needed support. I was so alone. Godfrey was fifty six then, so thirty years older than me, yes, but he didn't look it. He kept himself fit and I needed a father figure in my life. He was good to me. He started to take me everywhere with him, to places I'd never expect to visit, like Le Manoir and he didn't expect anything in return. It was only after three months that he started to stay over. I lived in a bedsit in Cripley Road near Oxford station. He said his marriage was dead and he'd get a divorce and marry me if I wanted. It wasn't a romantic proposal. You know the rest.'

'This Club, can you tell me more about it please? Did Godfrey continue to go after you were married?'

'Yes, but not often, just once a month and once or twice a month his closest mates would meet at The Tree at Iffley.'

'That's been helpful Mrs Price, thank you. I believe Mr Price's funeral is next week. I'd like to attend and show my respects.'

***

Alex arrived home to find a man with a camera peering through her window.

'Should I call Inspector Parker?' she asked. 'You know there's a murder hunt on.' The reporter grinned.

'You must be Alex Hornby. I'm Geoff Hunter from the Daily Mail. I was told that you found the body. Can you use your crime writing experience to suggest who did it?'

Alex's hand clicked the pen in her pocket. She disliked the Daily Mail. She loathed the way it stirred up prejudice against refugees, but she earned her living as an author and a lot of Daily Mail readers liked her books. She steeled herself to be polite but was determined to be ultra— careful about what she said.

'Okay, you can come in. I'll get us a drink.'

As she handed him a beer, she asked,

'What do you want to know?'

'I believe you found the body?'

'Yes, Thames Reach is a beautiful secret, in just a few minutes you can be on a delightful walk. That Sunday, I was walking from Sandford Lock to Abingdon along the Thames Path. I don't think the police would be pleased if I said much more.'

'How do you find this CI Ranjit Singh? Is he as good as your Inspector Parker?'

'Inspector Parker is fictional. Ranjit Singh has to deal with the real thing.'

'But do you think he's up to the job? Is he the right man to be in charge of the investigation?'

'What do you mean? I'll do you the favour of believing that you didn't mean that the way it came out. Just because there aren't many, if any, CIs with his skin colour, you suggest that makes him not a good investigator? If you want to stay and drink that beer, you have to promise me that you won't write any such insinuation.'

'Fair enough I promise. You're a writer. What angle do you think will interest Daily Mail readers?'

'That's easy— it's a 'Death in Paradise' kind of story. Our bit of the Thames is glorious and we are surrounded to the south by Radley Great Wood and Bagley Woods. We're only two miles from the Dreaming Spires of Oxford and we haven't seen a policeman here for years, until now that is.'

'So what kind of people live in Thames Reach?'

'You know as well as I do that some parts of England are socially exclusive in one way or another. Thames Reach is the opposite. Everyone is here but no one will boast about it. There are cleaners, office and factory workers, plumbers, electricians, mechanics and gardeners: there are nurses, doctors, teachers, librarians and writers like me. There's even a professional sculptor, a professional inventor, website designers and computer engineers. At one time, almost the entire Geology Department of Oxford University lived here. The academics are from Oxford and Oxford Brookes universities. The lab technicians and scientists work at Culham and Harwell and university spinoff companies. Add in postmen, policeman and lots of independent businessmen and women and you'll get that Thames Reach is independent and diverse. The housing stock reflects that.'

'Can you relate that to these murders? Give me some context?' asked Hunter.

'Godfrey Price lived on Abingdon Way. It's on an ancient route to Abingdon which boasts of being the oldest settlement in the country. No surprise then, that road has some stories to tell of highwaymen and kidnappers – are those days returning? Maybe your readers will enjoy a quote from 'Three Men in Boat' about the place where Frank Foreman's body was found. The pool beneath the weir where he was found is 'still', but it's deceptively still. Frank is not the first to have drowned there, hence the memorial obelisk on the weir. There's a good description of it in Jerome K Jerome's book.

"The pool under Sandiford lasher, just behind the lock, is a very good place to drown you in. The undercurrent is terribly strong, and if once you get down into it you are all right. An obelisk marks the spot where two men have already been drowned, while bathing there; and the steps of the obelisk are generally used as a diving-board by young men now who wish to see if the place really is dangerous."

Geoff seemed pleased and asked how he could find the obelisk to take a photo. Alex bought Thursday's Daily Mail and was pleased that Hunter had kept his word and made no insinuations about CI Singh. The editor had gone with '*Deaths in a Watery Paradise.*'

CHAPTER 16

THE GENTLEMEN AND WOMEN OF THE PRESS

THE PRESS CONFERENCE was packed. The Chief Constable led and was a strong and reassuring presence. She said that she understood why the people of Thames Reach were concerned.

'The village is a peaceful mostly crime-free place that has suddenly become the site of two deaths. The death of the director of Thames Reach Builders is being treated as murder. The death of Councillor Frank Foreman is being treated as suspicious. I note that one reporter' —looking at a pleased Geoff Hunter— 'has quoted from the Victorian travel book, *Three Men in a Boat*. The pond beneath the weir where his body was found has seen many deaths over the years. I'll hand over to Chief Inspector Singh who's in charge of the investigation.'

'The murder of Godfrey Price has added complications. Usually there are clues at a crime scene and we struggled, at first, to know how his body had got where it was found in the river a mile from Abingdon. There's been progress in our investigation. We now know that he was not killed there. We have good reasons to suspect that his body was disposed of in Sandford Lock. Using water from the sluice gates, it was swept downstream. So we are appealing to any member of the public who was near the lock on

Sunday May 24 between 6.30 to 8am to please come forward. DS Farr will give you contact details.'

'It's too early to discuss the second death, but we want to appeal for information regarding the kayak that was found with Councillor Frank Foreman. DS Farr can send you images of it and the place where he was found. Thank you for your co-operation.'

The Chief Constable thanked him and continued:

'This is an ongoing investigation and we are appreciative of the responsible way it has so far been reported. That really is helpful. We want to keep you informed as much as possible. We can't be certain that these deaths are related but the two men were friends. Anyone who has information that could assist us, please get in touch. Nothing is too small. We don't believe that the villagers of Thames Reach need be concerned for their safety but we do sympathise with all those who are grieving their loss. Frank's son James is on his way from Australia but Godfrey's son Kevin would like to say something on behalf of his family.'

The cameras focussed on Kevin who looked uncomfortable, but calm.

'My great-grandfather Alfred started Thames Reach Builders and my father Godfrey made it well known, not just in Thames Reach but throughout Oxfordshire. His standards of building were high and his staff respected him. He still had much that he wanted to achieve. His second wife, Samantha, is pregnant with their first child which he will now never see. My children adored their grandfather. I don't know how to explain to them that they will never see him again.

If any of you can help with information regarding his death, please help Thames Valley Police find out who did this.'

***

Given the lack of leads, Ranjit felt that the press conference had gone as well as it could in the circumstances. He realised that Alex Hornby was partly to thank for that. Flagging up the obelisk and the *Three Men in a Boat* quote had intrigued the press, as had the involvement of a crime writer. It had distracted them from the minutiae of the case and from him. They had allowed questions and many of them were about the boys who had found the body of Frank and some almost jovial queries relating to a crime writer finding Godfrey's body.

… He felt relieved, but how long would it last? And what would he find at home? He slowly turned the key.

Jia and the twins had watched the press conference. Roshan grunted his approval. Amber ran and hugged him. He had a whole evening off, looked at Jia and she nodded. A weight like an iceberg melted away.

***

With all the talk around the village, Sharon and Kevin could put it off no longer. The nursery sympathised with them. They understood that death is a hard subject to talk about.

'Honesty is best,' said the head. 'Try not to use euphemisms like *passed away*.'

That evening they sat the children on their knees and said:

'Your granddad has passed away.'

The children looked blank. Peter jumped down first and carried on building his Lego spaceship. Emily picked up her blue elephant and cuddled up close to her mother but closed her eyes.

Kevin turned his eyes away from his wife and from the problem, the invisible elephant in the room.

CHAPTER 17

A FUNERAL

RANJIT AND KATE watched the mourners enter St Lawrence's church. The press had agreed to stay away until the end. The family said they could be filmed leaving the church, but asked that their privacy during the service be respected. The press responded well and remained on the perimeter along with curious members of the general public.

An exception was made for a reporter from The *Oxford Mail & Times* because she was the contact Thames Reach Builders used when they had announcements to make. Kate noticed Alex talk to her and guessed they'd met when Alex was a freelancer for the paper. She and Ranjit sat at the back.

The church filled with people who'd known Godfrey all his life, plus representatives of firms he'd employed like solicitors, accountants, surveyors and estate agents. Then there was Mandy and workers at Thames Reach Builders and subcontractors including Marku. Kate pointed out several local politicians and even the local MP. She saw that Alex and the local reporter were sitting in the middle near to Angela, David and Carol. Kate observed that the front row was reserved for 'family' but they were either not welcome or preferred to be apart. Alex and David were the only non-whites in the congregation apart from Ranjit.

Once the hearse arrived, the front row was filled

by Godfrey's parents, Sam, Kevin, his wife Sharon and their children Peter and Emily aged three and four. Angela said the other man was a cousin. One absentee stood out – Margaret Pugh was not present at her ex son-in- law's funeral.

It was a surprisingly traditional service. There were two tributes one by Kevin and one by an old school friend. Their first choice had been Councillor Frank Foreman, but he was unsurprisingly nowhere to be seen, even in a spectral form, and neither was his absence mentioned. Kate and Ranjit listened hard. You often learned things about people at a funeral - things you'd never heard before. They were disappointed. Kevin talked about his father's support for the local boys' football club and of Oxford United where he had a season ticket; his love of golf but nothing at all personal. The only touch of that was the music they exited to. Godfrey was a fan of the Rolling Stones.

Susan and John Price, Kevin and Samantha shook hands with the mourners and invited them to the wake at a hotel by the Thames not far from where Alex had found the body.

When Marku emerged, Sam took him aside. He looked surprised.

Ranjit couldn't hear what they said but by now, he knew he could trust his sidekick to find out. Ranjit didn't want to intrude on the wake

As they walked over to say goodbye to Kevin, Sharon , Ranjit heard the children ask them,

'Great grandma, when's granddad coming back? I want to show him my space station,' asked Peter.

'Play grandad,' said Emily.

Ranjit approached the great grandparents. They were in their early eighties but the Spanish life obviously suited them because they looked physically fit. They looked as if they were struggling to accept their son dying before them. After expressing his sympathy Ranjit asked them,

'Will you be staying long?'

'I'll help for a while at the firm,' replied John Price. 'Once Kevin is confident he can manage without me, we plan to return to Spain. I want my grandson and his family to come to us for their summer holiday. They'll need to get away. I hope you find who did this.'

When he called on them the next day, they were open and informative about Godfrey's youth but were reluctant to talk about his marriages or his children.

***

Marku looked around the house. He ran a hand over the kitchen top.

'I built the walls, roof, guttering and drains - I've not seen the finished inside before.'

Sam looked surprised.

'Because of your part ownership of the land, I assumed you had met Godfrey here.'

'No - at the office.'

'Where do you live? Did your solicitors tell you that I wanted us to meet?'

'On a houseboat. *Sunny Days*. It near Iffley Lock. My solicitor tell me to see you but I didn't know how. So I see Kevin. But Kevin say Godfrey not told him anything. He think I am a liar. He want nothing to do with me.'

Sam had made sure Cleo and Alex were present. Alex thought that Sam was a good listener. She didn't interrupt although was shocked about some of the story. Alex asked,

'Do you have any idea why Godfrey didn't tell Sam about the joint ownership arrangement?'

Marku shook his head.

'I thought Godfrey is my friend - now not sure. All I want was to build a house for my wife and son to come here from Albania. Now, Kevin no want to use me as a subcontractor and f ...' and he sighed.

'Can we talk about this situation which isn't good for me or for you?' said Sam.

Alex thought Marku looked not just surprised, but shocked in a way she couldn't quite fathom.

'I need my rights.'

'At the moment, we share the rights to all the land on this plot and that doesn't benefit either of us. How about we divide it?'

Marku looked unsettled but not upset.

'How?'

'We cut off a plot at the bottom of the garden and make an exit onto St Lawrence's Road. That will be yours so that you can build your house there but in return you give up your rights to the rest of the land.'

Marku was silent.

'I am from Albania. Some things here ... how I know I can trust you?'

Alex said,

'We want to make an agreement that doesn't

involve paying solicitors for anything other than what is necessary. Your solicitor and Sam's solicitors will need to redraw the deeds. She'll have the deeds to this house and half the plot and you alone will have deeds to the rest of the land.'

Marku looked pleased but his smile faded fast.

'How we get permission to build on it?'

Sam looked at Alex.

'You have to fill in a planning application. The civil servant in charge of planning will discuss it with you. If your house design is in keeping with neighbouring properties, it should go through. Be modest, keep it to two stories and in a style similar to the rest of the properties. Locate it near to the fence adjacent with this property. That way you won't affect your other neighbour's light. Keep to the same building line and they should have no objection. If you satisfy the Planning Officer, your application will go to the District Council Planning Committee for approval. Sam won't offer any objections.'

'Kevin say he no longer give me work. I wish to do this but can't. How I pay for the materials.'

Alex looked at Sam and she nodded.

'It will take about six months for your planning to go through. You can submit plans now, even before the deeds are redrawn. Once the deeds are signed by both of you, Sam will be able to take out a mortgage on this house. She wants to separate a part of the house for her and the baby and let the rest of the house to have an income. Give her a quote on the work, but she can only pay you once the mortgage is approved. The sooner you divide the land rights the sooner that can happen.'

Sam was taken aback by Marku's response. The man was in tears. Sam went over to him and put an arm around him and said,

'I'm sure your wife and I can be friends.' He put his hands over his eyes.

'Ju lutemi pranoni mirënjohjen time më të thellë. I thank you.

I should have listened to that policeman.'

***

As the sun set, Alex sat in her garden alone with a drink, musing.

'… *I misjudged Sam when we first met.*'

She judged people by their books and Sam had none! Maybe things were changing because Sam had asked to read one of hers. She'd given her a copy of *Devil in the Library* which was set in the Bodleian. That was a start. Sam seemed willing to take advice now that arrogant edge had been chipped away. Could that have been defensiveness? After all, she'd deposed Carol and almost everyone in the village knew Margaret who still lived here. Until she met Cleo, she had no friends in Thames Reach. Sam was more thoughtful than she'd anticipated. The business with Cleo would be good for both of them and Alex knew they would grow in confidence. She asked Sam why she had no friends at the funeral. Sam looked guilty.

'I used to have a lot of friends from school and from work but Godfrey made a condition. If we married,

I shouldn't see them anymore. He said he was sorry but because he was older than me, it wouldn't look good and he didn't want temptations around either.'

Alex hugged Sam and said, 'He's dead and you can have all the friends you like here.'

Sam had looked as if burden had been lifted. It hadn't dawned on her that she was free to organise her own life.

'Once I'm earning money, I'll have a party but not yet. I want to live a normal life for the sake of the baby. I'm trying to get it out of my head that Godfrey was murdered because they say a mother's feelings transfer to the baby. I don't seem to be able to do it. I keep waking in the night hoping he died quickly but seeing so many possibilities. Who'd want to kill him? The police don't seem to know. I worry about whether I'm safe? What do you think?'

CHAPTER 18

LOVE, LUST AND LUCRE

SAM GOT IN touch with her bank and explained what she wanted to do. They agreed with her plans. As the outside of no 1 Abingdon Way would not be affected, she didn't need planning to separate her living space inside and a £100,000 loan secured by the house would be enough for that and for setting up the business with Cleo. Soon after the land deeds were signed, the money went into her bank account and she rang Burim Marku to start work. In the meantime, they heard nothing from the police but they had been seen at Thames Reach Builders and asking questions around Iffley.

***

The meeting began okay.

'The press conference went without a hitch and, so far, the reaction has been positive,' said Chief Superintendent Rayner.

Ranjit brought her as up to date as he could. He said that he'd talked to Angela and David after the funeral and his reaction to them was the same as Kate's. He didn't believe she'd kill her father and he had a cast iron alibi.'

'We know how the murder was done but not why. The three 'L's come to mind, Love, Lust and Lucre. I think we can rule out the first two so we should concentrate on the 'lucre' and Godfrey and Frank's business. I hope that following the money can lead us to the murderer,' said Ranjit.

'So you're telling me that all the investigations so far have led to dead ends. I do hope this line brings results. Time is of the essence, Chief Inspector. Don't feel that you can't ask for external help. I'm sure Scotland Yard will be happy to oblige.'

She'd been perfectly reasonable, so why did he feel that he'd been through a wringer. She was considering calling in help - the humiliation of it! Had the MET been right during all those years in not promoting him? He was clearly not up to the job. He knew the statistics. The first days were regarded as crucial. Had he missed anything? The Murder Book with all the interviews and evidence was growing longer and longer.

'If not the family, then *who*?

He decided to concentrate on Frank's murder. Both Godfrey and Frank were members of the Roof Top Club. What went on there? Was that the clue to the case? He asked Kate what she had found.

'They are all men, mostly property owners, builders, businesses and developers plus some councillors, Sir. It appears that women who run businesses don't get the same opportunities to network as the men and they haven't started their own. Not that many women would like the ambience of the club,' said Kate.

'The offshoot at Iffley?'

DC Jordan said, 'It was only Frank and Godfrey, and two Albanians, Sir.'

'Kevin wasn't included?'

'The booking was only for four, for a meal, but that doesn't mean that Kevin couldn't have turned up for a drink.'

'Do you know who the Albanians were? Was Marku one of them?'

'No Sir. Marku has a clean record but a reputation for having a hasty temper. The others were the Gega brothers and they are on our watch list. We suspect they could be involved in modern slavery but not so much in prostitution as in labourers.'

The two British men murdered and the two Albanians very much alive. Ranjit felt more optimistic.

'Get whatever you can on them and then we'll bring them in.'

'Where do they live?

'In Peachwood, the mobile home park on the Radley side of Thames Reach,' said Veronica Chen.

'But they have extensive property in Tirana.'

'Is there any evidence that TRB used them as gang masters?'

Thames Reach Builders was such a mouthful that the team had abbreviated it.

'No, Sir, but given that Frank Foreman was present, and they had just bought Radley Fields, maybe they were looking for cheap labour to develop it? The planning application was for two hundred houses. Usually TRB built up to twenty. This would take them into another league.' said Richard Smith.

'We need to talk to Kevin Price.'

***

Kevin looked annoyed and agitated.

'I hope you've come bearing news.'

'I'm sorry, Mr Price, but we need to ask you some questions about TRB,' said Ranjit.

'Aren't you satisfied by having turned this office upside down?'

'What was the purpose of the meeting between your father, Frank Foreman and Nikko and Luka Gega at The Tree at Iffley, a week before your father was killed?'

'I've no idea. My father was a control freak. Half the time he didn't even tell me what he was up to.'

'Could it have been about developing Radley Field? Your father transferred ownership of the field to you and Frank a few days before he was killed. There was another gathering at The Tree just before Frank's murder. Do you expect me to believe these events are mere coincidences?' said Ranjit.

'Frank was at that meeting. What did he tell you about it?' added Kate.

Kevin looked trapped.

'I've an appointment with a potential client in Abingdon in thirty minutes. I really haven't got time for this.'

'I suggest you come to the station after your appointment so we can continue our discussion, Mr Price,' said Ranjit in a matter-of-fact tone.

'I'll ask Mandy to ring them to say I'll be a bit late,' said Kevin changing his mind.

'You were going to tell us what Frank told you,' said Kate.

'Radley Fields is the biggest project we have

ever taken on. TRB only employs four full-time construction staff. We have a plumber, a chippy, an electrician and a foreman in charge of the bricklayers, plasterers and decorators. That works well when we are building single homes. We recruit extra casual labour for bricklaying, plastering, decorating and use Botley Plumbers and Cowley Decorators for larger projects. That keeps our overheads down.'

'But Godfrey had ambitious plans for Radley Field?' said Ranjit.

'Yes. He made promises to these Albanians. But I'm not sure I want to go ahead with this development. Frank was confident that he could get planning despite the opposition from the likes of the Gambles.'

'Look, I'm struggling to get on top of things here. Dad didn't consult me. He liked to give orders and expected to be obeyed. So I have my work cut out.'

'That sounds worse that I intended. He was a good employer. Mandy and the guys are well looked after and loyal. They've been with us for years, but dad wanted to be the boss. I want to be as good a boss as he was.'

'But I'd like to offer the land to a bigger national developer. I'll get a lot more for it, if I sell it with planning permission. That's my preferred option. I'd prefer to keep TRB the size it is now. I'm not as ambitious as my father. I want what do you call it? Work/life balance? I'd like to enjoy seeing my boys grow up and, if I'm honest, I'm not keen on upsetting the locals. I haven't got the stomach for controversy like Dad. But I may have no choice. The Gega brothers have a reputation. I don't want to upset *them.*'

Ranjit got up to leave and shook Kevin's hand saying,

'Thank you Mr Price. I appreciate you being *frank* with me.'

Kate wanted to smile at the unfortunate pun.

CHAPTER 19

NOSEY OR CURIOUS?

CLEO'S BABY WAS due in four weeks' time and she invited Alex and other neighbours to her baby shower. Alex looked at the invitation and thought - Father Christmas, Halloween and now baby showers – all North American imports. It's strange but not so strange that they involve people needing to spend money! Alex wasn't so much mean as curious. She was looking forward to seeing what changes they had made at number twenty-four.

As a writer, she had to be careful. She didn't want people thinking her nosey and intrusive. In her own eyes, she was curious and caring but that was what writing is all about thought Alex:

'Words and how they are interpreted. 'Nosey' or 'curious' depending on your perspective.'

Cleo's scans showed that she was expecting a daughter. What to buy? Babies had so many first size clothes that they hardly get used. Should she buy the next size or something more personal? In the end, Alex bought a baby book with a special cover made from multi–coloured felts. She'd remembered seeing one during Art Weeks, when local artists and craftsmen opened their studios. She rang Elaine, the artist who'd made them and asked if she still had one for sale. When Alex went to collect it, she knew that she would've loved recording her son's progress in a book like this. It would be something to treasure.

Cleo's reaction to it showed that she had chosen well.

Jo was absent - out playing squash. This was an all-female affair. As well as some old friends, Cleo had invited near neighbours. Alex was surprised to see Margaret Pugh. For a woman with dementia, she had done well. She'd bought a baby changing mat. Cleo poured wine for her guests but stuck to tonic water herself.

'It's not easy giving up alcohol altogether. *I DID it,* but I hope you lot bring champagne after the birth.'

Margaret followed the conversation without difficulty.

'In my day, they recommended Guinness to breast-feeding mothers.'

There was a ring at the door. It was Samantha, looking very pregnant.

'This is my first baby shower. Thanks for inviting me,' she said as she handed over her present, which was exquisitely wrapped. Cleo led her into the lounge and began to introduce Sam to her friends. Margaret glared at Sam. She got up and started to poke her in the stomach.

'You bloody whore. And THAT, I presume is your bastard.'

Sam burst into tears and Cleo looked at a loss. How had this happened? Alex knew that she had to handle the situation because Cleo couldn't. She went over to Margaret.

'You're upset and unwell, Margaret. Let me take you home.'

***

Alex sat with her for a while. Margaret looked fierce like a wrinkled Boadicea.

'I understand how you feel. Godfrey treated Carol and Angela abominably but, honestly, Sam is not a money-grabber. That was my first impression of her but, the reality is, that Godfrey started to date her at a vulnerable time in her life. Her father abandoned them when Sam was thirteen and, as she was an only child, when her mother died of a brain tumour she was absolutely bereft. She has one uncle but he lives in Spain. I believe Godfrey took advantage of that. He offered her support and protection although I expect you and I know what he really had in mind.'

Margaret said nothing but the anger drained from her face and Alex detected a look of regret. She left saying,

'If you need any help, Margaret, you know where I live.'

***

As she was such a close neighbour of Frank Foreman, Alex thought she ought to attend his funeral. The author had an added motivation. She was currently writing a chapter of *Bad Blood in Summertown* which included a mafia funeral. Alex hoped this would give her inspiration. Her novel was about what happened when a mafia family started to split and develop rivalries. Most of the clan were in Southern Italy but an offshoot in Oxford was running what looked like a legitimate business – indeed *was* a legitimate business. But it was also a convenient place to launder money. The family had become part of the Oxford social scene and lived in a basically honest way much like their neighbours. They simply turned a blind eye to the source of some of their income and lived as if they were pillars of society.

Having listened to Sam's story, Alex wanted Giovani to be a member of the Roof Top Club. When the son of the Godfather came to stay, everything unravels. This family split results not in angry words, like Margaret's, but in violence.

'It fits with my idea that the death of the godfather looked as if he had overdone the sex,' thought Alex.

Frank's funeral was also in St Lawrence's and, as with Godfrey's send-off, it was crowded with many of the same people, just fewer builders and more local dignitaries. Frank's son and his partner, two cousins and their partners and Kevin Price's family and Sam were seated on the front row, but there was no sign of his sister, Margaret.

Alex was surprised to see the Gega brothers. As someone with her ear to the ground, she had heard unpleasant things about these residents of Peachwood.

'Mm…' thought Alex. 'This is closer to my novel than I imagined.'

As she left the church she was not surprised to see Kate Farr attending.

'I'm not going to the wake. Do you fancy a drink at The Badger?'

***

Alex said, 'Families never cease to surprise you.

Frank's sister Margaret didn't come to his funeral.'

'Maybe she just forgot?' suggested Kate.

'I'm sure one of his friends and family would have brought her, if she'd indicated she wanted to attend.'

'Maybe she was worried about how she'd react to Sam?' replied Alex. She described Margaret's outburst at the baby shower and then changed the topic to the presence of the Gega brothers. Kate was allowed to say that they were persons of interest.

'If you hear any rumours about them, it could be helpful.'

Alex said that the village library manager lived on Peachwood, so she knew it well. Like Thames Reach, it had a strong community spirit and was quite friendly. The Gega's mobile home was large, modern and well-kept. It was somewhat set apart from the other homes, being the last bungalow before Radley Woods.

'There are two caravans parked next to it. They told residents that they were their holiday caravans, but walkers have reported noises coming from them,' said Alex.

'Thank you,' said Kate. 'Something useful always comes out of our meetings in pubs.'

'How's your Chief Inspector? I gather he was thrown in the deep end with this case.'

'I'm starting to feel sorry for him.' Kate looked as if she had surprised herself. 'He's cut back on the jokes targeting us so I can be more charitable. Ranjit is not bad at delegating and doesn't put people's backs up but it's hard to think of a more difficult case to solve than this one - two.'

'It strikes me that he'd be good looking if he smiled. Every time I've seen him he looks desperately serious,' said Alex.

'You're right. He tries to let his hair down a bit on a Friday evening at the King's Head. *'Hair down'* - strange I should say that. As a schoolboy, Ranjit had a top not and a turban – the lot. He has a picture of his family on his desk. His father looks very dignified in his turban.'

'But I don't think things are good for him at home. His folks expect him to attend extended family events and there are *lots* of them. None of us can take more than minimal time off, says me drinking with you.'

Alex raised a glass with one her hand but the other went to her biro which she clicked. Kate observed and heard this tic several times and wondered what set it off. If an author had an involuntary itch then pen clicking seemed to her the most appropriate.

'I sympathise with his family. My ex-husband was a doctor.' The pen clicked. 'It was fine before we had Marcus. He'd take a couple of hours off duty to meet near St Thomas's hospital. I had a career as a hospital administrator and he was supportive. Once we had Marcus there was no discussion, his career came first.'

'The world is still organised for men,' said Kate. Alex nodded and continued,

'We lived in Brixton. It's not far from St Thomas's in miles but even that distance was difficult with a baby, so during my maternity leave, our casual meetings stopped. I could have coped with that, but I expected him to spend at least some quality time with us. When we had holidays, instead of heading to the beach with us, he did research. It became as if we didn't exist. He was a good man but, if I was going to live the life of a single parent, why not be a single parent? I hope Ranjit's wife isn't on the same journey.'

Kate wanted to ask if there had been another man in her life since then but felt they hadn't known each other quite long enough to ask that question.

CHAPTER 20

EXPLOITATION

RANJIT ADDED PICTURES of the Gega brothers to the board. He asked Peter Jordan to report on his and Chen's observations.

'They are currently paving driveways. They each take a team to a site. There are three in each team. They all look Albanian and young – between eighteen and twenty-four. They take reasonable lunch breaks. Sometimes, the brothers go to the Co-op and come back loaded with sandwiches, chocolate bars, bananas and coke. On Thursday they went to the fish and chip shop and on Friday to the Red Lion in Radley. They all have iPads and play games with them in their breaks. They travel in two white vans. I'm concerned that they saw us following them to Peachwood yesterday evening. We may need to act quickly or they may move them.'

'It's likely that we can charge the brothers for employing illegal immigrants. My guess is that these men are not paid. The brothers probably imply they are giving money to their families in Albania.'

'Do you think the laptops food and accommodation is sold to them as pay?' asked Veronica.

'Tonight send a team to the caravans, bring them in and we'll ask them?' said Ranjit.

***

A daily national paper was delivered before breakfast and Alex's local weekly on Thursdays. She'd loved writing for *The Oxford Times* and admired the young people doing their best to keep it afloat given that it was no longer locally owned. She clicked her pen and then noticed the headlines, **Modern Slavery Case in Thames Reach.**

Alex turned the page to read the detail.

The men were charged this morning after raids at three properties at Peachwood mobile home park between Thames Reach and Radley. They appeared at Oxford Magistrates' Court yesterday afternoon.

Dressed in plain dark clothing, the two men spoke only to confirm their names at the three-hour long hearing.

Luca Gega, 39, of Peachwood Park is charged with one count of requiring six people to perform compulsory labour, and one count of arranging or facilitating travel of six people with a view to exploitation.

Nicoli Gega, 34, of Peachwood Park charged with one count of requiring six people to perform forced or compulsory labour.

The offences are alleged to have involved six victims.

Deciding if the case should be heard at the lower court or the crown court as each of the offences are 'either way' matters – meaning they could be heard at either of the two courts. Presiding Magistrate Anne D. Sutton decided it should be sent straight to the crown court.

She said that the magistrate panel would "decline jurisdiction" in the case, after hearing that any possible future sentence in the event of a conviction would be too significant for a magistrate alone to determine.

No formal pleas were entered at the hearing and all of the men have since been remanded in custody to next appear at Oxford Crown Court.

They would appear at the upper court on October 5, and no provisional trial date had yet been set.

Our reporter asked Chief Inspector Ranjit Singh if the arrests were related to the recent murders in the area. He replied, 'It's too early to comment on that.'

***

A cheerful looking Ranjit Singh emerged from the Chief Constable's office. Delighted by the modern slavery charges and the strength of the case, she followed him to congratulate the whole team, Ranjit's high didn't last .In private he was told that the progress on the murder cases seemed slow and he had only four or five weeks more with a full quota of investigators.

'Pressures on resources are great after the twenty percent reduction in staff. I won't have any other option. Jordan and Chen must be transferred to work on other urgent cases,' she said.

CHAPTER 21

THE LIGHT AND THE DARK MANICURED.

SAM'S MORTGAGE HAD come through and she wanted to thank Cleo and then Alex.

'How about we go for some spa treatments at Highfield House Hotel. We can relax and may get some ideas. They have a great fitness suite.'

Alex was pleased that Sam had moved on from Margaret's abuse and replied:

'As long as you let me be chauffeur to you beautiful pregnant ladies!'

The following week, Alex drove Cleo to no 1 Abingdon Road. She noticed that the security gates were wide open and tied back. They walked up the drive and rang the bell.

'What's this then?' said Alex pointing to the open gates.

'I don't want to feel afraid. They haven't found Goldie's killer but I need a life and it feels like I'm frozen– on edge all the time. I don't want to be cut off from the community. For our fitness business to have a chance of working, we have to look welcoming. I've asked Marku to remove the barbed wire. I may not have much experience but, in retail, I learned that a smile and genuine interest in your customers works well. I earned more commissions on sales than anyone else.'

Once inside, Alex saw a happy Burim Marku building the dividing wall to create a separate home for Sam. They asked him to join them for coffee before they left but he appeared uncomfortable sitting with them.

Alex asked about his family in Albania but, before he could answer, Sam said,

'You'll soon be able to meet them. I've invited them for a holiday.

They can get a three-month tourist visa. They'll stay here with me while the conversion is being done until the house is ready to Air B&B. Burim says his wife is a community midwife in Tirana. So her being here when I have my baby will be perfect. I don't have a mum and, if I'm honest with you, I'm nervous.'

Burim was not used to talking to women especially pregnant women, but given what he owed Sam, he tried some conversation.

'Elira can help me with the plans for our home. I have resident's rights, work and now I have property, my solicitor said she will have a case to join me. There's a shortage of midwives so that's in her favour.'

Alex asked him if he knew the Gega brothers.

'They are cheats and scoundrels. Many Albanians are poor but are prepared to work hard. Those criminals prey on them. They tell young men that they can work for them for a year or two and then set up their own business. Once here, they learn quickly that they are illegal and have been conned.'

'Why did those lads work for them and not complain to anyone?' asked Alex.

'The brothers make them afraid of the authorities.

They tell them that because they are illegal, they'll end up in jail if they say anything. Then they say that they'll pay their families in Tirana and when they return they will be rich. They *want* to believe the lies.'

'I feel bad because this was happening right under our noses. It makes me wonder what else we are missing,' said Alex.

When she got home, Alex started to write and then stopped to think. To write her kind of fiction she had to be sceptical and honest about the human condition. Recent events had brought it close to home. This was in no way COSY: it was distressing and horrific and it was happening to people she knew. Only a few months ago, Cleo and Jo had sat in her lounge and she'd wondered how to make crime-free Thames Reach sound interesting. This nosey crime writer had not expected modern slavery to be practised less than a mile from her house. She'd built a comfortable and successful life for herself since she moved here. She asked herself *'Am I deluded or do most people just turn a blind eye to evil?'*

***

After their facial, foot massage and manicure, they went for a healthy lunch under palm trees by the swimming pool. It had a roof, but the doors slid back so that most of one wall was open to the gardens.

'Do you think I should get Burim to do something similar to my swimming pool?'

Alex replied, 'The problem is the views. It looks like Godfrey preferred massive decking, concrete and bricks to plants. Why don't you plant some trees and shrubs?

Sam looked at Alex as if she was a genius.

'I love that idea, but it will have to be an easy garden because I can't afford to pay a gardener. Godfrey said that he wanted it paved so that the maintenance was low'.

'Can I make a suggestion? Invite the Gambles for tea. Ask their advice. Tell them you want to create a wildlife friendly garden. Explain that Godfrey hasn't left you money so it has to be easy to maintain. My guess is that they might even get the Thames Reach Rewilding group to help with the work if you cater for them. It could be like a work-party ending with a swim and a BBQ. And you could grow wisteria up the plastic pillars and have fairy lights after dark - that would make your entrance welcoming too. '

Sam looked happy. It sounded like a dream but she wasted no time and got on the phone. At first George sounded suspicious but he handed the phone to Carrie. Sam and Carrie were soon joking about the fortress being magically turned into the Garden of Eden. Altogether it had been a good day.

Alex was pleased she'd not passed on her dark thoughts to her pregnant friends. For the next generation you needed to be positive. You had to be prepared to work to make the world a better place.

'Perhaps that is why crime fiction is so popular,' she thought. *'Usually the crime is solved and justice is done. But that was not my childhood reality in South London.'*

She remembered the quiet dignity of her hardworking parents as they faced the cruelty of racism. They'd bought a house in Forest Hill just before she was born. Their struggle finding somewhere to live - the constant rejection they faced because of the colour of their skin - they put behind them. When her uncle had reported a crime, it was he who'd been treated as if he were the criminal simple because of the colour of his skin.

She was struggling with tough memories, when it came to her in a lightening flash— the certainty that the Windrush generation had changed Britain for the better. Their grandchildren should thank them. Alex went to bed early that night and slept well.

CHAPTER 22

THE OBELISK OF DEATH

PETER JORDAN HAD good news. His son was a sea scout. Their club house was close to Donnington Bridge. After the press conference, they checked all their boats and discovered that one was missing. There'd been no problem recovering it.

DI Jordan asked if they had CCTV but the answer was 'No'. This week, he arrived early to collect his son and met up with an old friend who suggested they cross the road to the boathouse catering for adults, which had a café. While downing his coffee, he noticed that they had CCTV. It was his inquiry after the Godfrey Price murder that had incentivised them to install it on their premises.

He asked if they had the recording from June 10 and took it back to the station. With Richard Smith, he pinpointed the evening before the discovery of Frank's body. They called Ranjit and Kate over to take a look. It was a rear-view image but judging from the man's clothes, his bulky size and severe hair style, they felt pretty certain that was Burim Marku kayaking downstream towards his houseboat.

Ranjit had stopped teasing Kate about her friendship with Alex Hornby. She always returned with useful information. Kate had told him what Marku said about the Gega brothers' trafficking enterprise. That was going to be very useful.

'I suggest we invite Marku here to talk about

the Gega brothers and how to recognise trafficked workers. It could lull him into believing that is the only reason for him being here. When we show him the CCTV recording, it will take him off guard. He's unlikely to have a fake reaction.

***

Kate arrived at no 1 Abingdon Road and asked Sam if they could borrow Burim for an hour. They would appreciate his help on recognising trafficked workers.

At the police station, they welcomed him effusively.

'Thank you so much for coming. We appreciate your help on this difficult issue,' said Ranjit.

Marku looked at him appreciatively. He remembered Ranjit's good advice: the advice he regretted not taking. For ten minutes that was what they discussed. Then Ranjit changed the subject.

'You live on a houseboat on the river near Iffley?'

'Yes, it's called *Sunny Days.*

'Do you own a kayak?'

Marku suddenly looked distressed. He tried to stop his hand trembling as he replied 'No.'

'DI Farr, please show Mr Marku the video.'

She turned her laptop to face him and clicked it on. The blood drained from Marku's face.

'I didn't kill him. It was an accident. I panic. I not take your advice to talk to Sam. I'm stupid. I think talking to a woman a waste of time. Godfrey told me that Frank Foreman sorted his permits. He not a friendly man but he was my only hope.'

'Bring Mr Marku a glass of water and we will start

at the beginning.'

Kate placed the water in front of him as Ranjit switched on the tape and recited the caution. He then asked Marku to begin at the beginning and tell them everything.

'I saw him. He walk along the path towards Thames Reach. He often drank at The Tree in Iffley with Kevin. He came near my boat. I invite him on board. I say flattering things—things Godfrey told me. I know he be reluctant but I say to him,

'You not driving - so one more pint won't hurt.' I try to relax him. He sat upright and uptight even with a bottle of beer in his hand. I say that I need his advice. "I have rights to land at 1 Abingdon Way. That was how Godfrey paid me. Okay. You know he liked arrangements like that which avoid the tax man?" Frank nodded so I continued. Godfrey say I can build a house for my family at the end of the garden. He say it convenient to have me on hand, because I'm a good worker. And he praise you. He said getting planning not a problem. You are his secret weapon. Mr Foreman, I need your help. Godfrey is dead and I don't know what to do. Can you help me? Please" '

'Foreman looked angry and threw the beer in my face and said,

"Why on earth would I do that?" He looked at me as if I am dirt.

Then he sneered,

"I voted Brexit because I'm fed up with your kind coming over here. I don't want you living in Thames Reach. GET OUT of my country.'

'He turned and started to leave. I was angry. He'd

insulted me and insulted my countrymen. We are not all like the Gega brothers. So I grabbed him and turned him round to face me. I want to tell him what I thought of him but he pushed me away. He lost balance. He fell backwards and hit his head on the stove.'

Ranjit suggested they take a break. He ordered tea for Marku and went to talk to his team. He asked Marku for the keys to *Sunny Days* so they could check out his story. He handed them over without any resistance. Soon Forensics examined every inch of the boat. Forensic photography revealed evidence of blood on the wood burning stove. They found a hair nearby which had Frank Foreman's DNA.

Kate took up the questioning. It was not difficult. Marku seemed relieved to have confessed.

'I panic when I see he is dead. It was near midnight. Po – sorry – that's Albanian.'

Marku looked distressed and put his head in hands and sobbed.

Ranjit was not used to a grown man crying in front of him. He couldn't help feeling sorry for Marku. He knew, from his own family, how difficult it is moving from one country to another even when you have command of the language. Marku was a talented builder and had a good grasp of English – not grammatical but he didn't need a translator. It was, nonetheless, obvious that English bureaucracy was like a foreign language to him—like internet coding, something beyond him.

'Take your time. Have some water and when you're ready...' said Ranjit.

'I walk to the boathouse at Donnington Bridge. I help myself to a kayak. It was there upside down on the slope. You know the rest. I saw the obelisk. I knew people had drowned there. I hope you think it a river accident.'

Ranjit charged him with stealing a kayak, of unintentional manslaughter and the unlawful disposal of a dead body. Ranjit decided that it was a jury's job to decide whether or not Marku was guilty of manslaughter, but he had confessed to taking the kayak and disposing of the body. The next day he was taken to the magistrate's court and sent for trial at the Crown Court. A date was set in early February. His solicitor asked for bail but it was refused. The reason given was that he could be a flight risk.

***

Jia noticed a difference in Ranjit that evening. He looked less pressured but as if something was on his mind. Her food soon had him in a better place and she asked about his day.

'It'll be in the newspapers tomorrow so I can tell you.' He told her about Marku.

'How did our parents manage, Jia? Interviewing Marku, I realised just how hard it is to change countries. He has marketable skills, is a hard worker and had a simple ambition – to provide a home and a future for his family. He got himself into this mess, not because he's a bad man but because he found the bureaucracy here impenetrable. He needed someone to navigate him through the system and picked on the wrong person.'

'I guess that's why we were under pressure to become doctors, lawyers and accountants. Our parents wanted us to be safe and secure and to know how this society works.'

'I must be a disappointment, but I hope not to you.'

The children were in their rooms. Jia leant over and kissed him. Everything felt in its place for Ranjit.

CHAPTER 23

INSIDE BULLINGDON

THE NEXT MORNING, Kate went to no 1 Abingdon Road to give Sam the news. She couldn't believe it and asked if she could see him. Kate explained how. After Kate had left, Sam called Cleo and Alex but only Alex came, as Cleo had started her labour.

They shared their disbelief that Marku killed Frank. Kate was allowed to say that Burim claimed it was an accident. They wanted to believe that.

'It sounds like he needs a good lawyer,' said Alex. 'I'll make enquiries.'

Then Sam pointed to all the building materials.

'What am I going to do? How can I finish this? My baby will be born in January.'

'Your son-in-law's a builder. Give him a call and tell him the news.'

Half an hour later Kevin joined them. His reaction to the news was less benign.

'At last! The police have finally pulled their fingers out and stopped harassing me. A bloody foreigner. No surprise there then. It wouldn't be beyond reason that he was involved in dad's death, too.'

Alex brushed Sam's hand and she got the message. Alex said,

'Sam's expecting your father's baby in January. You know that he didn't leave her any money so her idea was to create a small living space for her and their son and have an income by letting the rest. You can see Marku was doing it for her. Now he's on remand, he can't finish it.'

Kevin looked kindly at Sam. He went over to her and hugged her.

'Don't fret, Pet. I'll get the boys onto it. We have a job on nearby. I can't promise that they can come every day, but they'll fit it in around other jobs and I won't charge you. I see you have most of the materials you need. Give me the plans and we'll start next week.' After he'd gone Sam said,

'Thank you, Alex. Thank you for reining me in. I'm so relieved I can't believe it. Kevin was nice to me. I don't like his attitude to Marku but for once, he saw me as family. That is like a dream to me. I want more than anything for my baby to have a family - the family I never had.'

'Talking babies, what news of Cleo?'

***

Alex felt she was living in one of her stories. Thames Reach had become more like Morse's Oxford. Colin Dexter who invented the opera-loving detective had been so supportive when she started writing. She'd moved to Oxford with Marcus when he was nine, two years after her divorce. She and Andrew had agreed to sell their Brixton house and divide the proceeds. He was happy to live in a one-bedroom flat near the hospital but she wanted something bigger with a garden. That was when she decided to move near to Oxford. At that time, Thames Reach was almost totally white. There was an Indian and a Chinese takeaway, and a local shop and the post office were owned and run by South Asian ancestry families but she was the first black resident. It hadn't been easy but once she involved herself in local organisations, she was as accepted as much as recent white residents. You had to go back three generations, like the Prices and the Foremans, to be *totally Thames Reach*.

***

Kate and Alex had made it a weekly date to meet over a drink. After she told her the story of how she arrived in Thames Reach, Kate wanted to know how she became a writer.

'I took on an admin job at the university for just four days a week so that I could try my hand at writing. I began by writing articles for magazines and then I entered a short story competition. I couldn't believe it when I won. The money prize was small, but it gave me confidence and included an introduction to an agent.'

'Why crime fiction?' asked Kate.

'I went to a talk by Colin Dexter. He was almost eighty by then but was supportive. He offered to read and comment on a draft outline. I felt so lucky. *Agony in the Ashmolean* sold well. There was demand for more of Inspector Parker, so it became my genre. Marcus needed me around but by then, he had a teenage life of his own, so I took the plunge to become a full-time writer. I couldn't have done it when I was younger. My mortgage is now paid off, and my ex was generous with Marcus, so it wasn't financially risky. I supplement my income with some freelance writing and ghost writing and by taking in language students during the summer. I'm so glad I did. Once Marcus was at Uni, I felt lonely. My characters are great company.'

After getting home from The Badger, Alex got to work baking two lasagnes, one for herself and Sam and one for Cleo and Jo. She took that next door and admired baby Josh. Sam soon joined them. They told Cleo and Jo the news about Marku's involvement in Frank Foreman's death and said it would be in the national papers the next day, and so it was. When Cleo looked tired and Josh was sleeping peacefully, they crept out.

Over their lasagne, Sam asked if Alex would go with her to Bullingdon Prison where Burim was being held. She wondered if his wife knew. Alex suspected that he wouldn't tell her and wondered how she'd feel if a rumour reached her via Albanians living in Oxfordshire. She said,

'Burim is a proud man and pride has two sides. It can make you want to behave well, but it can stop you showing vulnerability or admitting to a mistake.'

***

The next day they were sat opposite Burim at Bullingdon Prison. He shared his side of the story and they were inclined to believe him. Sam asked about his wife.

'I don't want her to know. I don't want my family to know.'

Alex replied, 'I understand how you feel, Burim, but try to understand how your wife will feel, if you push her aside and don't let her help you.'

He lowered his head and gave the impression that he wanted to hear none of it.

'My life not worth living now.'

Alex looked anxious and thought: *'Suicide risk.'*

'Marku, listen to me please. You are at the bottom now and can see no way up, but you must have faith that things can get better. I have a suggestion to make.'

Alex's words pressed a warning buzzer. It was a reminder of his obstinacy, not going to visit Sam but instead trusting Frank. He wouldn't be in this situation if he'd been prepared to take women seriously. He lifted his head and listened to Alex's suggestion.

'It may help your trial if Elira is in the court. The jury will see that your story is sincere. She has the tourist visa.'

Then Sam smiled and said,

'How about she come here just before Christmas with your son as we planned? It'll be nice for me because Elira can help with the baby. You'll be doing me a favour.'

'Perhaps a good solicitor can get you bail. You've confessed and if your family are here and if you stay at no 1 Abingdon Way, we can give guarantees and that way they may let you out,' said Alex.

'Please don't be like Godfrey. Trust your wife. Let her help you,' pleaded Sam.

Alex promised to find him a good solicitor and Sam said she owed Burim for the work he'd done so could she do 'a Geoffrey' and pay the solicitor in lieu? Alex explained that as he'd confessed to disposing of the body, that crime would probably carry a four-year sentence.

'The barrister would need to convince the jury to believe you that his death was an accident - that is why you need a good lawyer to put your case. If the jury finds you not guilty of involuntary manslaughter, then you could be out in two years.'

Marku was in tears.

'I don't deserve your friendship ladies but my lovely wife – she do. I was stupid not taking the inspector's advice and coming to you Sam. I pay for my bad judgement. Now, I listen to you and take your advice.'

CHAPTER 24

ONLY CONNECT

THE ARREST OF Marku meant that Ranjit and Kate's reputation rose even though a chance encounter and follow up by DI Jordan had led to the arrest. The way Ranjit handled it, leading to the confession impressed most of his colleagues. But Peter Jordan felt overlooked and a bit resentful. Godfrey Price's murder was still a mystery, and Peter had no real confidence in Ranjit solving it. Was his career best served by asking to be moved on, or would Ranjit recognise his role in the arrest of Marku and recommend him for promotion? The Chief Inspector had, after all, noticed Veronica Chen who - because of him - had applied to join the CID. He decided procrastination was the best policy.

Ranjit fretted that Price's murder could become a cold case. The Chief Constable agreed to keep it live for another three months but moved Jordan and Chen on to other cases. Ranjit had to announce it to the team. He praised Jordan and Chen for their excellent work and wished them well. Jordan had been guarded lately as if something was wrong. Ranjit specifically invited him to the Plough in Wolvercote that Friday. He bought drinks for everyone and got them to raise a glass to Peter and thanked him for his sharp observation and action.

Ranjit had convinced himself that the two cases had been related but now that appeared unlikely. He interrogated the Gega brothers and they had alibis for the day of Godfrey's murder. It didn't have the hallmarks of a contract killing. He wished real life was like Alex Hornby's murder mysteries and that a motive for them wanting him dead would be discovered in a lightening flash of inspiration. Ranjit asked himself if he lacked imagination.

'Maybe that was his problem?'

He asked Richard to look again over TRB's business records and this time go even further back to see if Godfrey had had any serious complaints made against him. He went through the murder book to see if he had missed anything. But because of the other successes, the pressure was off him.

***

Life more or less went back to normal in Thames Reach after all the scandals of the past three months. The panic subsided as residents started to believe that Frank's death could possibly have been an accident and was, at the very least, involuntary manslaughter. Alex had finished her novel and was planning a launch. She'd promised to invite Kate. She rang her to reserve the date and had a pleasant surprise. Kate was living in rented accommodation in Botley, but said she planned to buy a flat in Thames Reach.

'What a turn up for the books. I saw it advertised by Hudson's but discovered that it's a conversion, by guess what builders? TRB! It's not far from you. They bought one of those cabin-like bungalows that were built when land was auctioned in the early twentieth century. The owner died so TRB demolished it and have built what looks from the outside like a house, but it's actually two flats. I'm buying the upstairs one. I love the light from the large windows at the back and I don't want a big garden. It comes with a patio space on the side next to what will be my front door, which is enough for me. The ground floor flat has the back garden.'

'That's great. It means we'll be neighbours. Shall we have our weekly pub meeting tomorrow?'

***

Over a drink at The Fox in Boar's Hill, Alex decided to ask Kate a question that had been bugging her.

'Is it a coincidence that both you and Ranjit moved here from the MET?'

'Yes but No.'

Kate looked at Alex's braids and continued,

'You don't need me to tell you that the MET has a culture problem. It's hard because so many cops, like me, want to do a good job. When you believe that you can change things for the better, you stay strong and stick it out. A relationship breakup meant I had to make changes and I needed to review my career. Not everything is hunky dory in the Thames Valley. I'm sorry to say that, even here, I've witnessed black and white boys on the same charge treated differently … BUT... I believe I can make a difference here and I had started to believe that I couldn't do that at the MET. Ranjit doesn't talk about his personal life, but I've got used to noticing body language. He had to put up with a lot of nasty culture in London so is better off here but I don't think his family feel the same way. '

'Thanks for being honest with me, Kate. I appreciate that. My parents didn't want me to feel afraid of blue uniforms. They thought I should be entitled to approach a policeman if I was in trouble. They stuck to it despite the experience of some relations. My mum is still alive. Dad died five years ago. He would've admired you and Ranjit. Maybe it was their attitude that has allowed me to be a crime writer. There aren't many non-white authors in the genre. Inspector Parker has some flaws but he's fundamentally a decent and clever man.'

Because Kate had been frank with her, Alex continued to open up to Kate.

'The Windrush generation believed they could change things but, for some of them, the Scandal was the last straw. They'd lived through decades of cruelty, insults, discrimination and the attempt to label their children as criminal, but through it all had remained positive. They wanted to create a better world for their children and grandchildren and they supported each other through the worst. They used music, dance, food and laughter to sustain them. But a big problem, when it came to contact with the police, was that Rastas enjoy a puff of weed.'

Alex paused to wipe a tear from her eye, remembering those gatherings when they tried to escape from the hostility and the damp grey reality of their everyday lives. Aware that Kate had watched her take out her pen, she deliberately put it back in her pocket.

'When the Windrush Scandal happened some people we'd met were deported after fifty years working and bringing up a family here. They felt they were victims. Let's face it, for many years, when black Londoners dared to complain about how the MET treated them, they were criticised as 'playing the victim card'. They were trying to bring enlightenment and change but it was the Windrush Scandal, that psychologically destroyed many of them. When you think you can change things for the better you stay positive but, if you can do *nothing*, that's the breaking point.'

'I'm glad we can talk like this,' said Kate. 'It'll be good to have someone to share the hard times as well as the good times.'

***

Alex went to tell Cleo that Kate would soon be a near neighbour. She had the impression than Cleo had been appreciative of the non-aggressive way she'd treated people even though she was involved in a murder investigation. Alex decided to use the news as an excuse to call on Margaret. She hadn't seen her for a while.

When Margaret opened the door, it came as a shock to her. Last time she'd talked to her, she looked ten years younger than her age but now she appeared every bit of her seventy-seven years. She looked desperately ill. After talking about Kate, Cleo and the baby, Alex made a suggestion.

'Couldn't Carol come to live with you? She's on her own and *you're* on your own and now Godfrey has died, she may like to move back to the village.'

Alex felt like pinching herself. Was she becoming

an interfering busy body? She told herself that she couldn't help herself because Margaret looked in need of TLC. To see her now, no one would believe that this woman was once a marathon runner. The suggestion seemed to appeal to Margaret until she said the word 'Sam' with a bitter tone.

'Seriously Margaret, Sam is a decent person. Her situation is not so different from Carol's, because Godfrey has left her no money or life insurance. I understand how you, Carol and Angela felt when he married a twenty-five year-old blonde. I too was guilty of stereotyping her as marrying him for his money, but I was wrong. I've no doubt that the financial stability he offered was an attraction, but she had no support and he used that. I've no idea if he had genuine feelings for her, but she seemed to have loved him. She's beginning to understand herself better. She might even begin to see the situation through your eyes. Why don't you and Angela try to forgive her?'

***

A month later, Carol moved in with the help of Kevin. Soon afterwards she was seen planting bulbs in the front garden. George Gamble walked past her house to access the woods and noticed her in the garden. He stopped to talk to her. They'd been at school together. He commented on the garden and suggested she get involved in rewilding. He even told her about what they were doing at the fortress. Carol looked interested.

Alex invited Carol, Margaret and Cleo for coffee. The baby was fussed over and Cleo asked Carol if she would like to hold her. Those beautiful eyes connected. She was still dressed dowdily, but Alex took pleasure in seeing Carol come out from the hole she had dug herself in. Margaret looked happier but there was obviously something seriously wrong. When she asked her, she shrugged it off as 'getting old.'

***

Franklins succeeded in getting bail for Marku on condition that he stayed at no 1 Abingdon Road and wore a tag. That meant that Elira and their little boy arrived early in December. TRB had finished most of the work dividing the property. Some decorating on the new staircase and in the playroom was needed and Marku took that on.

Sam tactfully left them alone in the large part of the house and retreated to her wing. Elira spoke English but not little Luca. Sam suggested that he go to the nearby nursery so that he could become bi-lingual. Marku said,

'That's a wonderful idea, but we not afford it. It is hard for me to work. People know what I did.' He lifted the edge of his right trouser leg to show the electronic tag. The lovely Montessori nursery around the corner was not cheap.

'If I pay the fees, can you accept that as wages? I can't do anything formal. This has to be about friendship. That is where I hope my baby will go if

Cleo and my business is a success. That won't be for a year so. In the New Year, I'll need to let this house in order to have an income. Until then, instead of rent, you can maintain and clean it for me. If I buy our food how about you cook it, Elira?'

'I don't know how we'd manage without you, Sam,' said Marku.

'You make a wonderful mum', said Elira.

She couldn't have said anything that would make Sam happier. She wasn't sure how to be a good mother, but that was what she most wanted in life.

The arrangement pleased them all. Marku and Elira spent some time on the houseboat. Because he wasn't working, Marku was able to repair and paint it with a view to letting it. Alex said she would keep an eye on it for them while Marku served his sentence. Elira made new curtains and cushion covers and hung two mirrors to make it appear larger. They invited Sam Alex and Cleo to have tea there to proudly show them the results of their work.

'It's like a TV makeover,' said Cleo. 'You'd better come and advise me, Elira. We've still got plenty of work to do on our house.'

If the trial wasn't looming over them, they would've been happy. Luca distracted them. He was shy at first and took a week to settle in at the nursery because of the language. Once he met the animals and had a session in the adventure playground, he became eager to go there each morning. He'd come home with new English words and games.

For Sam it was her best Christmas ever. She gave a party and invited all her old school friends and her new friends. Alex suggested that she invite Margaret and Carol and she did. They didn't come but they replied in a friendly manner. Kevin and family dropped in for a while. He was surprised by how well his son Ben and Luka played together as if they had known each other all of their short lives. Kevin kept away from Marku but at least they were in the same house. At the end of the evening his attitude to Marku had thawed slightly. His wife, Sharon, commented on how different the house felt, how much more warm and welcoming. The ground floor was no longer a vast empty space. It was smaller now and had colourful cushions on the settees and Gabbeh rugs. There was even a new piece of furniture—a bookcase.

CHAPTER 25

BIRTHS, MARRIAGES AND DEATHS

SAM'S BABY ARRIVED a week early. She was home after two days and wondered what on earth she'd have done if Elira wasn't there. She cried a little.

'On my own – how would I have coped?'

Luca loved the new arrival.

Cleo and Alex arrived to meet him.

'What are you calling him?'

'I should call him after his father to remember him. Godfrey is such an old-fashioned name. That's why I called him Goldie. So that is what I'll call his son, Goldie. He's my golden boy.'

The doorbell rang. 'Surprised' was an understatement of Sam's reaction to her visitor. Angela had been visiting her mother and grandmother when she heard the news from Alex. The author had asked her to forgive Sam. She'd told her what she knew and Angela agreed that they should put the past behind them. She was, after all, Goldie's aunt and the baby had done her or her mother no harm.

When Angela arrived bearing gifts, Sam broke down in tears.

'I so want him to have what I didn't –a family. Thank you. Thank you so much for coming. I love the present you sent and so will Goldie. I've already hung the Winnie the Pooh mobile over his cot. '

Margaret had written on her card.

'I loved playing Pooh Sticks at Sandford with my children and grandchildren. The current is fast there.'

***

A week later, Alex had a surprise phone call. Margaret asked her if she could come for tea. Carol had gone to London to stay with Angela. Alex congratulated Margaret on helping Carol.

'Three months ago she rarely went out, let alone go on a trip to London.'

'Yes, that's why I've asked you here. I want to confide in you. You've been a good friend and I trust you. Alex, I don't have long to live. I have put my affairs in order. I have left everything that Carol, Angela and Kevin need to know in a file in that desk. Here is a letter which I want YOU to open but not now. I've put a date on it.'

Alex looked at it. ***To be opened on February 10.***

'Can you give me a solemn promise me that you won't open it before then? I explain everything in that letter which I'd like you to share with Carol, Kevin and Angela.'

Alex promised but left confused. This all seemed far too well thought through for someone with dementia. But Alex believed her when she said that she didn't have long to live. A few days later, she was surprised to see Margaret getting into George Gamble's car.

***

Alex was at a loss. *Bad Blood in Summertown* was in

the hands of the book designer. It was as if she had lost a child. She needed to think about her next book. She was jotting down some tempting ideas when involuntarily she had a vision of Margaret. She was driven by an impulse - a necessity to visit her. She was disturbed by it. It felt like a physical jolt as if Margaret had just died.

She crossed the road and knocked on the door, but there was no answer. She walked around to the back garden and peered in through the patio doors. Margaret wasn't there. Carol was in London with Angela so Alex decided to ring Kevin, thinking he would probably have keys to his grandmother's house. She googled Thames Reach Builders and found their number. Mandy answered.

'Is Kevin there? This is urgent.'

Kevin came quickly and ran upstairs to the bedroom. Everywhere was neat and tidy and there was no sign of his grandmother. It was February 9th. Alex explained to Kevin what his mother had said to her.

'She made me make a solemn promise that I wouldn't open this letter before February 10. What do you think I should do?'

Kevin rang Angela in Brixton. She was upset and said she would get time off work and drive Carol back in the morning. Kevin looked worried but said,

'It's just few hours to wait. Angela aims to be here at 8am so I suggest we come here as soon as they arrive.'

Alex told Kevin where to find the file. It was mostly documents relating to her will. That and the deeds to the house and other relevant documents were held by

Challenor and Jones. In the event of her death they should contact them.

***

Kevin, Carol and Angela were seated around her dining room table when Alex opened Margaret's letter. The A4 envelope contained two letters. The first one was addressed to Alex to be shared with Kevin, Carol and Angela when convenient. The other was addressed to DI Farr.

Alex read the letter out loud.

'I am sorry to have deceived you. I do not have dementia. You will recall that, five years ago, I suffered a heart failure. I told you that it was minor and that it may not affect my life expectancy. That was not quite true. The doctors told me that I probably had five years. Nine months ago at a check-up, they were honest with me. I had surprised them but nonetheless I could die at any time.

When Godfrey married Samantha, he bullied Carol to favour Kevin and Angela in the divorce settlement and take only a little herself. If she didn't agree to his suggestions, he threatened to cut both of them out of his will. When he did that to Angela anyway, despite his promise to Carol, I was upset and concerned. (I love you both, Kevin and Angela. If you love me, please be good friends.)

When I heard that Samantha was expecting, I knew that, if she had a son, it wouldn't be long before Kevin could receive the same treatment as Angela. Godfrey didn't confide in you, Kevin, and he wouldn't tell you if he altered his will. Think about it with an open mind, Kevin, and you will know that I write the truth.

I had not long to live, so I came up with a plan. I decided to kill Godfrey while his current will stood. To avoid suspicion falling on me, I acted in strange ways and appeared confused so that people thought I had dementia. It was not hard. I simply had to occasionally look blank as if I was somewhere else and behave erratically. I could act fairly normally when talking about the past because it is the short term memory that goes first. The ruse worked because Inspector Singh did not suspect me. I think DI Farr was not quite so convinced, so I would like you to pass my confession to her.

When you read this letter, I'll be dead. I had a friend help take me to Switzerland to Dignitas. He is a friend indeed. You will see in my will that I have left my house to Carol and Angela. Kevin has inherited Thames Reach Builders so his future is secure. I have a few investments and those I am leaving to George's organisation for rewilding Thames Reach. I like the idea of doing what I can to leave a healthier environment for my grandchildren.

Forgive my deception. I did it out of love for you. It's lucky that I don't believe in hell or as a murderess that is where I'll be heading. I hated what Godfrey was doing to the three of you and that was why I could do it. Now I am facing death, I'm not sure that he deserved to die but I am content that your futures and my grandchildren's expectations will be bright. To your friends, you can explain it as me losing my mind. I'm hoping the police will regard it as murder with *'diminished responsibility'*.

Alex, thank you for helping me see sense regarding Sam. Her son will receive £1000. Kevin's children' legacy is in the will. If there is anything in the house that you like to remind you of me, I'd like Carol to give it to you.

It was signed *Margaret Elizabeth Pugh* and dated February 7, 2023.

Alex rang Kate and suggested she come immediately.

Kate opened Margaret's confession.

The first part was a repeat of sections of the letter to Alex, Carol, Kevin and Angela. In addition, she explained how she had done it.

'The phone call to Godfrey was from me. I asked him to come to my house and told him not to tell Sam. I had some information he needed to know urgently. I didn't want to tell him on the phone and I didn't want it traced back to me. He was doing some questionable things with the Gega brothers so I guessed he would come. He said, 'Can't it wait, its only 5 am?'

'That's why this is a good time. No one will see us if we go to the yard before six,' I said. 'Tell Sam there's a problem there and you won't be lying. Bring your gate keys.'

He was annoyed, but he came. I told him that I had it on good authority that the Gega brothers were taking advantage of him. They had hidden a cache of drugs in the yard. I said that I couldn't tell him who told me because they'd bought heroin from them and had followed them to where it's hidden. So I said,

'If we go there, you'll know if that's right or a red herring. I hope I'm wrong. I haven't forgiven you for how you treated my daughter but you're the father of my grandchildren, so I don't want to see you lose your good reputation or end up in prison.'

He muttered that I'm demented but he was convinced enough to drive us there. We went into the office. From when Carol and he were together, I knew where Mandy kept her insulin. While he fetched the keys for the warehouse from the rack in his inner sanctum, I took out four insulin pens. I followed him towards the door. I had prepared. Take a look at the camel coat in my wardrobe. On the inside, you will see that I sewed a very large pocket. In it I placed a hammer. I had tied a thin piece of cloth over it, in the hope that it could disguise the cause of the injury. I hit him hard with it. He fell hitting the edge of the filing cabinet. I thought he was unconscious.

At that moment I heard a noise outside. It was Carrie. I crouched beside the cabinet. Godfrey started to twitch. Fortunately, Carrie was soon gone and I gave him the first doses of insulin. But he surprised me. He got up and staggered towards me. I ran out towards his car and opened the driver door as if to get in. He lunged at me but I moved to the side so that he fell forward into the car, and I injected him with two large doses of insulin in the back of his left leg.

It was hard moving him. He was a dead weight. I brought the trolley and pushed him onto it. I covered the body with cardboard – to disguise what it was - and then with tarpaulin and tied a rope around it. Then I wheeled it down to the lock. That was the easy bit, because not only was the yard trolley battery powered to enable heavy materials to be moved easily, but there's a downward gradient toward the river. I had problems manoeuvring it onto the bridge at the bottom of Sandford Lane. For a horrible moment, I thought that I would have to abandon my plan and drop the body in the cut. I found a log to stop it rolling back and looped the end of the rope over the rail. It felt like an achievement when I was able to push it through the pedestrian access on to the level bridge. All the training to run the London marathon was not for nothing but my end was hastened by the effort. Despite wearing a TENS machine, I felt a sharp pain in my chest and had to sit on the trolley for a few minutes. I saw a jogger on the Thames Path ahead and worried that it was getting too late.

My husband and I had a boat and I knew how to operate the lock. The lock was almost empty so I tipped his body into it. I opened the gates on the Abingdon side. Then I opened the sluice gates on the Oxford side, so that the force of the river water would take the body a long way downstream. I hoped it would end up opposite the Thames Path near the Global Retreat because that way, it could be a few days before it was found. That didn't happen. Returning the empty trolley to the yard only took five minutes but it felt like forever. I expected to meet dog walkers or cyclists who would not forget seeing an old woman with a builders' trolley.

As I write this, I would not have the strength to do what I did. At the time, I knew it had to be then or never. I didn't want my grandchildren to see me arrested and die in prison awaiting trial. I contacted Dignitas before I killed Godfrey. They gave me an idea of the likely progression of the disease. There would be a time when I'd find it hard to get there. With George's help, I'll be able to fly to Switzerland. For the record, I didn't tell him that I was going there to die, only to find out what it was like and to consider it. No one else knew of my plans. I alone was Godfrey Price's nemesis.

It was signed Margaret Elizabeth Pugh and dated 7 February, 2023.

Kate didn't for a minute believe that George was unaware of her intentions, but she believed the rest. She took the letter to the station. They collected the coat from the wardrobe. There was a pocket inside and a hair from Godfrey was found in the camel pile and a trace of his blood on the sleeve. From what they already knew, it added up. She hadn't used a car but a powered builder's trolley to transport the body, so she didn't need a key for the large gate to the bridge. It was hard to believe that Margaret was responsible but the evidence seemed conclusive, so the case was closed.

Ranjit's first year with Thames Valley had been eventful and sealed his reputation. He decided to walk the Thames Path between Iffley and Sandford to see it in a different light. He diverted onto a trail beside the cut, as it was quieter. He came to a tree on the top of which was a cormorant with wings spread wide looking down on him looking up. *What pride!* Godfrey was proud and had become a powerful man used to everyone doing his bidding. He would not for a second have considered Margaret a threat.

Ranjit was starting to understand George Gamble's

perspective. Proud and arrogant men had destroyed so much of nature. Today everything looked calm, beautiful and peaceful but in the winter, where he was walking, it would be flooded. Nature has a way of answering back. Our actions have consequences.

Ranjit stopped for a coffee at Proof Social next to Thames Reach Builders and glimpsed Kevin Price coming out of his office. His experience of the Prices made him examine his own life and he realised how much he had neglected his family. He resolved to put that right. After coming to Oxford, Jia and he had begun to drift apart. She would soon have a demanding new job and needed his support if they were to stay strong.

At work, he now had confidence in his team. He wanted to make a success of his career but not if it meant cutting out his family. Ranjit looked at the river flowing effortlessly. His life needed to be like that.

To demonstrate his resolve to improve the quality of their family life, he insisted on taking a holiday. *Maybe he should take them to Amritsar, to the Golden Temple?* Roshan and Amber had not been to India. They could also go on Safari in the Corbett National Park and connect with nature.

He took out his phone and messaged Jia. Telling her that he'd booked a long weekend next month, when he would work at the Community Kitchen at the Gurdwaha in Southall.

***

While there with Jia by his side and his father looking on, he felt the desire for a fairer society. It connected him to his father's faith. The food was free to all and rich and poor ate side by side. He took charge of the catering at the Gurdwaha on the anniversary of his grandfather's death. His extended family were present and helped and he experienced a deep sense of belonging. Serving food was like serving up love. It took his mind off violence and prejudice.

Alex had a plot for her next novel.

The murderer would pretend to have dementia.

EPILOGUE

THE MARKU TRIAL

Burim Marku was found guilty of stealing a kayak and disposing of a body but was found not guilty of involuntary manslaughter. He was sentenced to five years in prison. Sam and Alex were regular visitors. While in prison, he let the houseboat and Alex helped him obtain planning permission for a two-story house fronting St Lawrence's Road. He decided that he would return to Albania and set up a holiday business there, so sold the plot with the planning permission. When he was released on parole after two years, there was a tidy sum in the bank. Once his sentence was complete, he started a business in Albania. He kept the houseboat so that his family could visit England regularly, where he could do occasional work to supplement the family income.

***

Marku remained grateful to Alex and learned to confide in her. He had considered suicide before she and Sam visited him in Bullingdon prison. 'We Albanians like the Ancient Greeks. Epicurus say, 'The art of living well and the art of dying well are one.' I thought myself an honourable man and when confronted by my flaws, I didn't want to live with them.'

ACKNOWLEDGEMENTS

Halcyon Leonard: for suggesting the part of Oxfordshire where we live could be a good location for a 'whodunit'

John Argyle: volunteer lock keeper and chair of the Friends of Kennington Library - for invaluable information on the locks and river.

Haldi Sheahan: for an idea with legs and her unstinting support.

Alex Green: Editorial assistant at Claret Press for his good advice.

Oxford eBooks: for their efficiency and proficiency. A delight to work with this, for me, local publisher.

Elizabeth Vetta: for the cover painting.

Philip Hind: for the cover photo.

Antonia, Alexandra and Anastasia Vetta: for the illustrations.

Andy Ffrench, Peter Tickler, John Argyle and Beth Langley : for endorsing Current of Death.

The organisers of the Oxford Indie Book Fair: for their support and encouragement.

ABOUT THE AUTHOR

FOR TWENTY FIVE years, Sylvia Vetta has written the life stories of others - 120 Oxford Castaways for *The Oxford Times* were turned into three books. Following that she wrote three novels inspired by real events and real people. Her memoir, *Food of Love: cooking up a life across gender class and race* is highly praised.

CRIME FICTION IS a new venture for her so she has rooted it in an area she knows intimately.

Sylvia's memoir published by Claret Press

Food of Love cooks up a life across gender, class and race.

With food comes love and with love comes hope.

Milton Keynes UK
Ingram Content Group UK Ltd.
UKHW032044180324
439698UK00001B/23